VICKSBURG

ଔଔଔଔଔଔଔଔ଼ଔ଼ଔ଼ଔ଼ଔ

In Memory of
Horace Redman
By Clarke County State Bank
ଔଔଔଔଔଔଔ଼ଔ଼ଔ଼ଔ଼ଔ

VICKSBURG

•

Kent Conwell

AVALON BOOKS
NEW YORK

© Copyright 2005 by Kent Conwell
Library of Congress Catalog Card Number: 2004098748
ISBN 0-8034-9718-0
Published by Thomas Bouregy & Co., Inc.
160 Madison Avenue, New York, NY 10016

PRINTED IN THE UNITED STATES OF AMERICA
ON ACID-FREE PAPER
BY HADDON CRAFTSMEN, BLOOMSBURG, PENNSYLVANIA

To Shea, who likes a good mystery.
And to Gayle, my wife,
who adds a delightful mystery to my life.

Chapter One

Voltaire wrote, 'the most uncommon sense of all is common sense,' of which, I'm reluctant to admit, I displayed a considerable lack of by not remaining in bed that Sunday morning.

When the phone rang, I should have turned my back, pulled the covers over my head, and slipped back into the welcome arms of Morpheus.

But I didn't.

Still, I could have avoided all the trouble by simply refusing Jack Edney's request to drive him from Austin, Texas to Vicksburg, Mississippi for his father's funeral.

But I didn't.

And I don't know why I didn't.

Maybe it was because I felt I needed to put some much needed space between me and my Significant Other, Janice Coffman-Morrison, or maybe because I couldn't help feeling sorry for my old friend, Jack, who, within the last few weeks, had found himself saddled with a broken arm when he drunkenly stumbled off the stage during his after-hours comedy routine at the Red Pepper Club on Austin's Sixth Street; a reassignment by a vindictive school administrator to teach at the Alternative School in Austin; an ex-wife who hated him; bill collectors hammering at his door; his driver's

1

license suspended by the Austin Police with the sworn vow that he would get it back when the cow jumped over the moon; and now had been kicked in the teeth by the unexpected death of his father.

Good, bad, or otherwise, Jack was on a roll.

Other than escaping Janice's increasing penchant for control that had resulted in several rancorous arguments between us, the only consolation I had for the inconvenience of a few days off work without pay and the boring rigors of an eleven hundred-mile round trip on the Interstate was the self-satisfaction gained from helping a friend because he could not drive with his left arm in a shoulder-high cast. But I figured if the situation was reversed, Jack would do the same for me.

Maybe.

That modicum of conceit lasted until we reached Shreveport, Louisiana.

Jack, the burr-headed, ever-bubbly comedian and storyteller, had been strangely silent, uncharacteristically silent since we left Austin just after midnight Sunday. All he had done was continuously jab an emu feather inside the cast on his arm to satisfy the itching. He was putting more mileage on that feather than I was on my Silverado pickup.

"You'd be surprised how it can get in there and stop the itching," he explained after climbing in my pickup. He held up the eighteen-inch long white feather with the double plume. "It's a tail feather of an emu," he added with the condescending tone of a feather connoisseur. "They're the best, you know. Very flexible, which lets me almost reach around my elbow. Isn't going to bother you, is it?"

I shook my head. "Have at it."

Ruefully, I reminded myself of my remark later when we strolled into a McDonald's for breakfast in Tyler, Texas. With Jack and his feather following, I headed for the counter. I heard giggles, and when I looked around, Jack, his face intent with concentration, was parrying and thrusting the emu feather in and out of his cast with the dexterity and vigor of a fencing master wielding a rapier.

"Why didn't you leave that thing in the car?" I whispered, embarrassed by the curious looks thrown our way.

"Because my arm itches even in here," he whispered back.

I just shook my head and tried to ignore the amused looks folks were giving us. I reminded myself that after all, Jack was my friend. And he needed help, feather or not.

Later, as Shreveport, Louisiana fell behind us, dark clouds rolled in from the southeast in escort of a gray wall of rain. That's when Jack cleared his throat. Eyes straight ahead, he cleared his throat and said, "Tony, I got a confession."

I stiffened. I hated it when out of the blue someone started a conversation with "I got a confession." I glanced at him. Now, Jack had the habit of running his tongue back and forth between his gums and lower lip when he was nervous. And right now, his lower lip was undulating like waves in the Gulf of Mexico during a hurricane. Warily, I replied, "Confession? About what?"

He hesitated, then blurted out, "I had another reason for asking you to drive me over here."

Keeping my eyes on the road ahead, I frowned, growing even more wary. "Another reason?"

Jack tried to scoot around in the seat to face me, but he could only manage to turn halfway for the cast on his left arm struck the back of the seat. He poked the feather down his cast and scratched. Apologetically, he explained, "Truth is, Tony, I asked you to drive me over here because I need your help. I think someone killed my old man. I can't believe the fire was just an accident. I want you to find out the truth."

Ahead, chain lightning exploded, its zigzag branches lancing out across the dark sky from the sizzling white trunk—a portent of the next few days, but I was too simple-minded to see it.

The unexpected confession raised the hackles on the back of my neck. He had lied to me. He had deliberately taken advantage of our friendship. I shot him a fiery glance.

Before I could utter a blistering retort, the rain hit, a blinding gullywasher that slammed into the windshield, rocking the truck and cutting visibility to less than thirty yards.

Gripping the wheel tightly, I peered into the silver curtain battering at us, my blood boiling with righteous indignation. I resented anyone exploiting me, manipulating me. And right now, I told myself, that's exactly what Jack Edney had done—just like Janice Coffman-Morrison. My sense of self-esteem was sorely offended by the idea someone would think I was so shallow that I could be manipulated.

Jack saw the irritation scribbled across my face, so, brows knit with remorse, he tried to placate me. "Okay, Tony. Now, I suppose if you really, really wanted to, you could make an argument that I took advantage of you. I—"

I looked around at him in mock surprise. "That's mighty big of you, Jack. Mighty big, seeing that's exactly what you did."

He pleaded. "Look, Tony, I was desperate. Besides, you're the only one I can trust to find the truth. Don't misunderstand. I wouldn't dream to presume on our friendship by asking you to look into this without pay. I'll pay you twice your hourly rate."

The rain continued battering the windshield as I digested Jack's explanation. My initial anger at being lied to was suddenly tempered not only by my curiosity, but also by the unbridled avarice $150 an hour can generate.

Keeping my eyes on the road ahead, I sneered, "Where are you going to get that kind of money?"

A tinge of pink touched Jack's plump cheeks. "I know this sounds pretty cold, but my old man was well off. I figure my share of his estate to be a couple million or so."

I whistled silently, any degree of wounded self-esteem at Jack's deception now completely suppressed by full-blown greed. After all, I told myself in an effort to rationalize my complete reversal of righteous indignation, I'd always wanted to visit the historic city of Vicksburg and the battlegrounds. Now I could not only pick up $1,200 a day, but also fulfill a dream of several years.

By the time we crossed the Mississippi River and rolled into Vicksburg just after 10 A.M., the rain, along with my temper, had diminished to a foggy drizzle.

There's an old superstition that cats have nine lives. It should be modified to say cats and Tony Boudreaux have nine lives, for later, during my second hour in Vicksburg, I used up my first life. By the time the next few days were all over, I would be down to my last one.

Chapter Two

The first half-hour in town we spent trying to find the home of Jack's deceased father.

"What do you mean, you don't remember where his house is?" I demanded as we pulled to the curb on a hill overlooking the river. "You were born here. You grew up here." Below, the foggy drizzle obscured the western side of the slow-moving river.

All Jack could do was shrug. "I haven't been back in twenty years. Things have changed," he replied, looking over the hills of the old city. "I don't remember all of the streets. Try over there, Old Town," he said, pointing to a street that sharply descended a steep hill.

Muttering a curse, I followed his directions. Finally we stumbled across the old house, a nineteenth-century two-story Victorian with a front and side gallery. Two Cadillacs and a blue Ford F150 pickup were parked in front.

I shivered as I studied the house and grounds. Giant magnolias with plate-sized white blooms like the eyes of ghosts, and massive oaks from which dangled witch's fingers of Spanish Moss surrounded the house, and the fine drizzle falling from the leaden clouds enveloped it all like a malevolent, wet cloak.

"Spooky," I muttered, parking my Silverado pickup next to the Cadillac.

"Home," Jack mumbled. He drew a deep breath. "Do me a favor, Tony. I haven't told my brothers and sister what I suspect. I don't want to tell them anything until I'm positive. After all, I could be wrong. I hope so."

I studied him a moment. "So, what about me? Am I here for any reason? Or just a means of transportation?"

"My old man restored Model Ts and Thunderbirds. I figured you might be a friend who volunteered to drive me over so you could take a look at them." He gave me a conspiratorial grin. "Isn't that what you PIs call a cover story?"

I rolled my eyes. I wasn't crazy about cover stories. Seems like someone always forgot a critical point at a critical time. "Why don't we just keep it honest. I drove you over because you can't drive. On the other hand, I wouldn't mind taking a look at the old cars. I might even be interested in buying one, if you decide to sell any." Grabbing my windbreaker, I opened the door and stepped out into the thin, but steady drizzle. I looked up at the old house. There was an ominous presence about the white structure. I shivered once again.

The second half-hour in town, I met the brothers and sister—WR, Stewart, and Annebelle—in the parlor of the house.

To say the family was simply dysfunctional would not do justice to the word. Dysfunctional with uninhibited sociopathic tendencies might be a more apt description, and not even that portrayal would encompass the full scope of their dysfunction.

"Tony's interested in one of John's cars," said Jack.

WR Edney shook my hand, but the scowl on his fleshy round face told me the handshake was a meaningless gesture. His coal-black hair was parted on one side and slicked down across the other. He looked greasy. "I don't know that we're going to sell any of John's cars," he said to Jack as he shook my hand, his voice a growl.

Confused, I glanced at Jack, who explained. "Nobody called the old man, Dad. We all called him John."

Wearing a gray uniform of the Riverside Bread Company, Annebelle shook her head, her frizzed hair bouncing like jello. She pointed the half-full glass of bourbon in her hand at her brother. "You don't talk for all of us, WR. If Jack's friend, Bobby, here wants to buy a car, they're ours to sell."

"Tony," I said, reminding her of my name.

She shrugged. "Oh, yeah. Okay. Sorry."

Annebelle certainly knew how to make a newcomer feel welcome. She set her bourbon on the coffee table. I noticed the marble top was Italian, the coveted Carrara marble. The only reason I recognized the elongated crystals that formed interlocking gray formations was because my Significant Other back in Austin had the same type of marble in every room.

And that's why I winced when Stewart, the other brother, propped his feet up on the coffee table and leaned back on the Victorian couch. "You just back out of this, Annebelle. You aren't even in the will." His voice was high and thin with effeminate nuances, almost identical in timbre to his sister's. His head was as bald as Annebelle's was frizzy.

A solid fifty pounds overweight, Annebelle struck me as an enemy to be avoided, not to be aggravated as her brother seemed to be doing to her. She ran her fingers through her kinky hair and jabbed a thick finger at him. "You just wait until you hear the will, buster. I told you John put me back in. He shouldn't have cut me to begin with." She leaned forward, her black eyes fixed on Stewart. "But someone told him lies about me."

Stewart snorted again. He and WR were built much like Jack except they had the height by several inches.

Annebelle sneered. "That's why I asked William Goggins to come over this afternoon, so you can hear for yourself."

WR raised an eyebrow. "You're getting things backward, aren't you, sis? The memorial service isn't until this evening."

She shook her head. "Forget it. I'm tired of arguing with you two. Besides," she added, turning her attention back to Stewart, "if John was going to cut anybody out of the will, it should have been you. You're the one who put the family to shame in New Orleans."

With a furtive glance at me from the corner of his eyes, Stewart stiffened and his face turned crimson. He snarled, "You got no room to talk, you and that roommate of yours. Everyone knows what's going on between you two."

"Why you—" Annebelle bared her teeth and started around the coffee table after Stewart.

He leaped from the couch. As he did, he brushed the end table, knocking a Tiffany lamp to the heart pine floor, smashing it into tiny pieces.

"Hey!" WR yelled, and quickly stepped between the two, pushing each of them backward a step. "This isn't solving anything. Both of you just back off."

Annebelle slapped his hand off her chest. "You don't go pushing me around, big brother," she snapped.

WR threw up his hands and stepped back. "Forget it then. I'm just trying to calm you two down. That's all. You want to fight, have at it. Just leave me out of it." He backed away while Stewart and Annebelle glared at each other.

I glanced at the multi-hued shards of glass scattered across the floor, wryly wondering if the lamp would come out of Stewart's share of the estate.

Jack shrugged at me and nodded to the door.

"Where are you two going?" Annebelle demanded as Jack opened the door.

Without looking at her, Jack replied over his shoulder. "To show Tony the old man's cars while you three calm down."

"Look all you want!" WR shouted. "We're not selling them!"

Annebelle yelled, "Yes, we are!"

And then the closing of the door mercifully muffled the shouts from inside.

I glanced down at Jack. "No offense intended, but I can see why you haven't been back in twenty years."

Jack simply grunted.

A short distance along a red-brick walk winding through the bougainvillea and azaleas were the remains of the old man's workshop and garage where he had restored his vehicles, its blackened walls still standing. A few feet beyond the skeletal walls sat a cavernous metal building, the cream-colored side next to the burned garage blackened from the heat generated by the fire.

Inside were thirteen Model Ts and seven Ford Thunderbirds, 1955s and '56s.

We spent the next half-hour looking over the restored automobiles. I shook my head in amazement as I admired a 1925 Model T Runabout with a green body and black fenders. "This was some hobby your old man had."

"Yeah. Expensive, but he could afford it."

I circled the Runabout, imagining Janice's surprise if I pulled up in front of her condo in it. "How much are these things worth?"

Jack shrugged. "Beats me. The old man used to trade with Doc Raines down at the Vicksburg Auto Parts. Doc specialized in antique cars. He was down on Washington Street. I don't know where he is now, or if he's even still alive, but I wouldn't mind knowing what they're worth." He glanced back at the house and arched an eyebrow. "I got a feeling I'm not going to be able to trust my brothers or sister."

With a chuckle, I said, "Well, the parts house is a starting place, both for value of the cars and your father. Point me towards Washington Street, and I'll try to run this Doc Raines down while you can get back inside and catch up on old times with your family."

"I can't wait," Jack replied, his words oozing sarcasm. He

pointed west. "Washington is by the river. It runs along the levee. Can't miss it."

As we left the garage, a Lincoln pulled up in the drive. A dignified man in a three-piece suit and carrying a briefcase stepped out.

"Uh oh," Jack muttered.

"What?"

"Dollars to doughnuts, that's John's lawyer. The one Annebelle sent for."

"How can you tell?"

"He looks like a hungry shark."

I studied the attorney as he strode briskly along the sidewalk. Lifting an eyebrow in appreciation of Jack's perception of the man, I noted the protruding nose beneath a receding forehead and above a receding chin. I couldn't have labeled him any better.

As Jack hurried after the attorney, I climbed in my Silverado and headed for the auto parts store, and the first attempt on my life.

Chapter Three

Washington Street was one of the main thoroughfares back in 1860s Vicksburg. Down through the decades, the narrow dirt street had been paved with red bricks, and while the Civil War facades of most of the buildings were maintained, the interiors had been modernized into bright and airy facilities replete with central air and heat.

Janice would be dazzled by the restoration.

I scowled when I realized I had unconsciously thought of her. I'd wanted to put her out of my mind. Truthfully, she was a fine woman, but she had the disconcerting tendency to be domineering, a trait she inherited from her only living relative, her Aunt Beatrice Morrison, the CEO of one of the largest distilleries in Texas. However, one accolade I had to hand to both the ladies—one they certainly deserved—was that neither of them could, by any stretch of the imagination, be labeled clinging violets.

And while I'm bogged down in the throes of truth, I admit I had no one to blame but myself for I knew just how independent Janice was when our relationship began. In fact, that was one of the several qualities that drew me to her.

But now, after a few off-and-on years, I felt as if I needed a break from her. Maybe each of us needed a break from the other.

Yet, here I was, still thinking about her. What was it the curmudgeon said about love, 'a temporary insanity cured by marriage?' That was one cure that could wait.

After half an hour, I found the parts house on Washington Street.

The nearest parking along the curb was a few doors down. The fine drizzle continued. About half of the buildings on either side of the street had porches extending over the sidewalk. One of the exceptions was the red-brick building next to the parts house, a future museum according to the red-on-white banner in the window.

As I emerged from under the porch next to the museum-to-be, a muffled cry sounded from above, and an eighty-pound bag of cement slammed to the concrete sidewalk four or five feet to my right, exploding into a billowing gray cloud that covered me from head to toe.

With a shout of alarm, I leaped back under the porch. After my heart slowed from the heart attack range, I tentatively stuck my head out from under the portico and looked up. A construction worker wearing a hard hat was peering over the parapet of the building, a worried look on his face. He waved at me. "Hey, sorry, pal. You all right?"

Pausing a moment, I gathered my shaken senses. "Yeah. Yeah, I guess so."

The man shook his head. "Jeez. Scared me to death."

I arched an eyebrow. "Didn't do me any good either."

A wry grin curled his lips. He waved and disappeared.

A hand touched my arm. "You okay, mister?"

Still half-dazed, I looked around into the concerned face of a black man about my age. I nodded. "Huh? Oh, yeah, I suppose so. That was close."

He cut his eyes to the parapet and gave his head a shake of disgust. "Them construction workers. Seems like they never pays no attention to what they're doing. They always causing problems. Sometimes I wish we never done started redoing all them old buildings. I was sure glad when they finished with our block."

I glanced up and down Washington Street, noting the reconstruction under way in the next block.

"You sure you all right, mister?"

I drew a deep breath. "Yeah. Yeah." I extended my hand. "Thanks, buddy."

"You're mighty welcome. Sure don't like to see you tourists hurt. Bad on our pocketbook," he added with a broad smile. He nodded to a small restaurant on the corner beyond the parts house. "I own that place. The Daily Grind, I calls it. Name's Isaac Wilson. You feel like a coffee or something stronger to perk you up, it's my treat."

Brushing the gray powder from my windbreaker and washed-out jeans, I declined. "Thanks." I nodded to the parts house. "But, I've got to see a man about a Model T."

I paused before entering the parts house. Emblazoned across the glass door in a semi-circle was VICKSBURG AUTO PARTS. Beneath it was the slogan, "We Do Antiques Before They Do Us." I arched an eyebrow, having absolutely no idea what the comment meant.

On the outside, the building appeared as it must have in the days of the Civil War, but inside, it was pure twenty-first century and bustling with activity.

An older man who looked to be in his late sixties or early seventies with a round head, a round nose, a round belly, and wearing a green uniform with the name "Doc" on the pocket, greeted me with an affable smile and an amiable manner. "How can I help you, friend?"

I nodded to the nametag. "You must be Doc Raines."

"You found him, you lucky devil," he said, laughing. "What can I do for you? I have a completely restored Model A roadster on sale this week. Only sixteen thousand. Perfect for a Sunday afternoon drive with the little lady. You can see it right out back."

I introduced myself. "I'm not a customer. I'm really just doing some legwork for a friend, Jack Edney. Maybe you know him?"

Doc's grin faded. "Yeah. I know Jack. Or I should say I remember him. Haven't seen him in years, but I know his . . . I mean, I knew his father. Shame what happened. His father was a good friend. A real craftsman when it came to Model T and Thunderbird restorations."

"That's why I'm here. The family asked me to see if you could line up customers for the cars." It was a white lie, but I had to start somewhere.

A frown wrinkled Doc's shiny forehead. "That's right. They're probably going to want to sell them, aren't they?"

"That's what I figure. I would."

The store owner frowned and shook his head. "Sure hate to see that collection broken up. JW did a fine job with them."

"JW?"

"The old man. John Wesley Edney. Real religious. Straight-laced, in fact. Named after some Methodist preacher back in the 1800s."

"I thought he was called John."

"That's what the kids called him. He preferred JW. Why I can remember—"

A young clerk interrupted the owner, and before Doc could take up his story where he left off, I spoke up. "The family will probably ask you for appraisals on the vehicles."

A grin played over his face. "Not to brag, but I'm the best in town." He winked. "Only one, in fact."

I laughed. "I don't know much about old cars. Ballpark figure. What do you figure they're worth?"

Doc suddenly became sly. "Hard to say."

"I won't hold you to it. We just need a ballpark figure. Somewhere to start."

"Well, depending on several factors, you could probably

get between fifteen and twenty-five thousand for the Ts, and twenty-five up to fifty for the Birds."

I whistled in genuine awe. "Not bad."

He grinned slyly. "Not bad at all."

"Did you know him very well? I mean, Mr. Edney."

"JW? Sure. He was one of my best customers and best friends. We went to some car shows together. In fact, the last one was at Lafayette, Louisiana just last Thursday and Friday. We'd usually drive down and share a room. That's what we did this time." He shook his head. "But all this is sure a surprise, I tell you."

"A surprise? How's that?" I tried to be nonchalant.

Doc eyed me curiously a moment, then explained. "JW was a careful man. This morning's newspaper said it was an accident, but he wasn't the kind to have an accident. He was too cautious, too deliberate." He shook his head. "Goes to show you. You never can tell."

"Just what did happen?"

With a shrug, he said, "Story that came out in the newspaper was that the cleaning solution caught fire. That was something else that surprised me."

"Why is that?"

"Well, sir, JW usually cleaned parts with ACL cleaner because it wasn't very flammable. For some reason, the last time he ordered cleaning fluid, he wanted naphtha. About a month ago." He paused. "Well, he didn't order it. Stewart, the next to the oldest, did." He shook his head. "That was a surprise too." He paused and chuckled. "Seems like I seen a lot of surprises lately."

"Oh?"

Doc nodded emphatically. "Stewart and JW had a big falling out some time back. They stopped talking to each other, so naturally, I was surprised when Stewart ordered it. But, I figured the two had made up, and JW just hadn't said anything about it."

I nodded my understanding, and he continued. "Anyway, the fire marshal said the fire started from a spark when JW was cleaning his fireplace tools." He shook his head and clicked his tongue. His brows knit in sadness. "He polished those brass fireplace tools just like his cars."

A red flag popped up in front of me. Before he could continue, I broke in. "I'm sorry. I didn't understand what you said about the fireplace tools."

His smooth forehead wrinkled slightly. "Huh? Oh, I said that the fire marshal figured the fire started from a spark when JW was cleaning his fireplace tools."

"Brass tools? You're sure?"

He nodded emphatically. "Yeah. Brass. JW claimed they once belonged to Andy Jackson."

I frowned. "Jackson?"

"You know, the president. Old JW found them at a weekend flea market over near Monroe, Louisiana. Personally, I figure some slick hustler fed him a smooth line." He paused and studied me. "You a friend of Jack's?"

"Yeah. We live in the same apartment complex in Austin."

"What's Jack doing now? I haven't seen him in . . . let's see . . . must be over twenty years. He was just out of high school when he left."

"He's a school teacher."

"Really?" The rotund storeowner raised his eyebrows. "Would never have guessed that. What line of work are you in?"

"Security," I replied, preferring not to go into specifics. "Jack broke his arm and couldn't drive. So—" I shrugged. "I'm just giving him a hand."

"Well, when you see him, tell him to drop by. Be good to see him—or any of JW's kids for that matter."

"You got it." Then I remembered the little runabout. "By the way, one of JW's Model Ts is a 1925 Runabout. What do you figure a good price would be on that?"

He arched an eyebrow. "For you?"

"It's cute," I replied.

A frown of concentration wrinkled his forehead. "Oh, I'd guess fifteen, maybe eighteen. The only problem with that one is the gas tank leaks. As far as I know, JW never got around to repairing it."

"Well, they're all nice looking cars." I glanced out the window. "Lot of construction out there."

"Yeah. Keeps things torn up. But we're lucky on our block. All the construction is complete."

Before I could reply, three customers entered. Doc nodded to them. "Been good talking to you. Tell Jack I said hi."

"You bet. And you might put out the word about the old cars."

"Sure thing."

I paused just outside the front door and looked up and down the wet sidewalk, considering Doc's last remark. *All the construction is complete on our block.* Same remark Isaac Wilson had made only minutes earlier.

If the construction was complete, then what was the hard hat doing on the roof of the soon-to-be museum with a bag of cement—in the rain?

I walked along the outside edge of the sidewalk back to my pickup, all the while keeping a circumspect eye on the parapets overhead. If another bag of concrete headed my way, I wanted to see it coming.

Safely behind the wheel of the Silverado, I jotted the essence of my conversation with Doc Raines on one of the ubiquitous three by five cards I always carry. I learned long ago that sometimes individuals say and remember different things at different times. I'm reconciled to the fact I'm not swift enough to keep everything in my head, so I rely on the cards to help keep everyone honest and me thinking straight.

An added benefit of the cards is that I can rearrange them in any manner, often permitting me to spot an angle or perception I had overlooked. Technology is good, but there are times when pencil and paper work better.

I glanced up to see a bright red Dodge Ram 1500 pickup rumbling my way. As it passed, I spotted the construction worker who had dropped the cement sitting behind the wheel. The white logo on the side of the pickup was shaped like a shield with the words "Rebel Trucking" in the middle of the logo.

After the pickup disappeared up the street behind me, I slipped the cards in my shirt pocket and peered through the windshield, studying the restored buildings around me. As both Doc Raines and Isaac Wilson had said, on this block, all refurbishing did appear to be complete. The adjoining block was still under construction. I studied the pile of powdery cement on the sidewalk. By now, the drizzle had soaked the cement, and tiny, gray rivulets ran off the sidewalk into the gutter.

I asked the question of myself again. If all the construction had been completed on this block, then why was the construction worker on the roof with a bag of cement in the rain? And, why didn't he clean up the mess he'd made with the cement? I looked back up at the empty parapet. Then I thought back over Doc's remarks about the fireplace tools.

After a few seconds, I muttered, "Jack, what have you got me into?"

Chapter Four

Pulling up in front of the late John Wesley Edney's home,
I spotted Stewart next to the new Lincoln, gesticulating
wildly at the attorney behind the wheel. He shot me a mur-
derous look.

As I mounted the steps onto the porch, I heard shouting
and cursing behind the closed door. That's when I noticed
that instead of a doorbell, the old mansion had a bell pull.
Grinning at the novelty, I sharply jerked on the brass knob,
and from inside came the ringing of a bell. I opened the
door slowly and stuck my head inside. "Am I interrupting
anything?"

Jack, WR, and Annebelle turned to stare at me. Jack
waved me in with his emu feather. "Nothing except a family squabble."

I figured my smartest reply was silence.

WR snorted. He ran his thick fingers through his thinning
black hair. "I wouldn't call it a squabble. War's a better
word."

Annebelle stepped forward and jabbed a finger at him.
Her lips stretched tight over her bared teeth. "You heard the
will. I told you John put me back in." She folded her arms
over her chest and glared at him. "And there's nothing you
can do about it."

WR shook his head and looked at me, his eyes revealing his frustration. His jowls flopped when he shook his head and spoke to Jack. "I don't understand it. John said nothing to me or Stewart. And he always did." He crossed the room to the cherrywood sideboard between the two French doors on the outside wall. He grabbed a fifth of Jim Beam bourbon from the several bottles of liquor and splashed some into a glass. He downed it in one gulp and poured another. He glared over his shoulder at Annebelle. "How'd you know he made a new will?"

A smug grin ticked up one side of her lips. "None of your business, but for your information, he called me on the twenty-fourth just after lunch. He was going to meet with his attorney."

He shook his head. "I don't understand none of this."

Her voice laced with sarcasm, she sneered, "Obviously, he didn't tell you everything, WR. That's probably one of the reasons he made Goggins executor instead of one of us."

He stared fiercely at her. "So you say."

She snarled at him. "Yeah, so I do say. Did he tell you he was leaving us that property south of town?" Before WR could reply, Annebelle answered her own question. "No, he didn't. You and Stewart were as surprised as me when Goggins read that provision in the will. You can't deny that."

He shot Jack a fleeting glance, at the same time as running his tongue between his bottom lip and gums, the same nervous habit as Jack. He sneered. "That swampland? It's practically worthless. John had a chance to unload it on some sucker several years ago and didn't do it."

Don't ask how I knew, but WR was lying, maybe not about the fact JW didn't unload it on some sucker, but that the land was worthless. I would have bet my life savings that he was lying, all $683 I had in the bank.

At that moment, Stewart slammed the door open. His round face was dark with anger. Beads of water glistened on his bald head. Cursing, he strode directly to the sideboard and downed several gulps directly from a bottle of Johnny

Walker Red scotch, spilling some on the pink silk shirt stretched over his ample belly.

He glared at Annebelle. "I don't know how you did it, you—" He spit out a few words that my grandfather would have taken a club to me if I'd said them to a woman. "But, I can tell you one thing, I'm not taking this lying down. I'll drag you to court if I have to."

With a smirk on her face, Annebelle plopped down in one of the richly upholstered wingbacks with the ornate rose wood trim. It groaned under her weight. "Take your best shot."

Stewart sputtered and stammered. He looked at WR. "Well, aren't you going to say something?"

The older brother barked. "What do you want me to say?" He glared at Annebelle. "You want me to say she outfoxed us? Okay, she outfoxed us. I don't know how, but she did."

"I didn't outfox anyone. John just came to his senses, that's all."

Jack spoke up. "Listen to me, all of you." Before any of the three could object, he continued. "First, I'll admit I don't deserve a full share like the rest of you."

Stewart pointed at his sister. "She sure don't deserve a full share."

Jack waved his hand. "Hold on, hold on. I'm not arguing any of that. All I'm saying is that bashing each other won't help. We're family. We're all that's left now. Let's talk about this sensibly. I haven't been around much, but—"

WR sneered. "You finally said something right."

Ignoring his older brother's sarcasm, Jack continued. "But, if you don't think I deserve what John left me, tell me what you think I deserve."

His last remark silenced his brothers.

I was impressed with Jack's plea, his sincerity, although I did have to suppress a smile as I watched him standing there with his arm awkwardly fixed in a cast at shoulder level.

Annebelle spoke up. "None of that, Jack. You take what the old man left you."

Reluctantly, Stewart agreed. "Yeah, but—" He struggled

to find the right words, but when they didn't come, he shrugged.

Jack glanced at me. I nodded to the adjoining dining room. This family melee was driving me crazy. I cleared my throat. "If someone would point me to the kitchen," I said, addressing the four of them, "I could use a drink of water."

WR nodded to the sideboard. In a gruff voice, he said, "Here's whiskey if you want some."

"Thanks. Maybe later."

"I'll show you," said Jack, leading the way through the dining room. As he passed the dining room table, he picked up a handful of unopened sympathy cards.

Once in the kitchen, I drew a glass of ice water from the refrigerator as Jack tried awkwardly to open one of the envelopes. Seeing his frustration, I opened it for him.

"Thanks." He read it. "It's from one of John's friends."

I looked down at the other cards. "They haven't been opened."

Jack shrugged and gave me a sheepish look. "What can I say? My family—" He struggled for the right words. "My family is, well . . . you can see, they're . . . different."

He would get no argument from me on that remark. No wonder his father named someone outside the family as executor. Without replying, I opened the other cards for him, glancing at the return address if one was there. From the eclectic sources of the cards, I guessed John Wesley Edney was not only religious, but civic-minded also. There were cards from churches, fraternal organizations, city agencies, and various businesses as well as from numerous individuals. One that caught my attention was from the Madison Parish Ornithological Society, headquarters, Richmond, Louisiana.

"Here," I said, handing him the stack of open cards. "Read them at your leisure. But now, we have to talk."

He arched his eyebrows in curiosity. "About what?"

I sipped the water and glanced in the direction of the parlor. "First, you're not to repeat to anyone, not even your brothers or sister what I'm going to tell you. This is strictly between the two of us for the present. You understand?"

A frown wrinkled his forehead. "Yeah. I won't. Don't worry. So what's up?"

I leaned forward. "I think you were closer to the truth about your father's death than you know."

"Why do you say that?"

I lowered my voice. "Something is going on. I don't know what."

"You find out something from Doc?"

"First, someone either tried to kill me or scare me." I quickly told him about the bag of cement. "I think maybe it was meant to scare me, but I'm not sure."

"Couldn't it have been an accident?"

"I don't think so. According to Doc Raines, all the construction in that block was complete. There was no reason for anyone to be on the roof, especially with a bag of cement and in the rain."

"So, what does that have to do with my old man?"

"I'm not sure, but one thing Doc said struck me as odd. I need to verify it with the police, but according to the record, your father started the fire when he struck a spark cleaning his brass fireplace tools with naphtha."

Jack stared at me, the blank look in his eyes testifying to his lack of comprehension. "So?"

I groaned. "So, Mr. College-Man School Teacher, a.k.a. comedian, brass does not spark. It's too soft. There's no way he could have caused a fire with naphtha and brass." I hastened to add, "Now, I'm not saying he might not have struck a spark some other way, but one fact is certain. He did not strike one with brass."

Jack's eyes grew wide. "You mean, maybe my hunch was right? Somebody might have killed John?"

"Maybe. That's why I want you to keep quiet," I replied, thinking about my old friend on the Galveston Police force, Ben Howard.

Chapter Five

I'd worked with Ben several times over the years, first when he was in Austin, and later in Galveston. He was a cigar–chomping curmudgeon. Despite his grating personality and deliberate bad manners, Ben Howard was a thorough and determined investigator. His bulldog tenacity to ferret every little detail of a crime earned him promotion after promotion.

Over the years, he became a fixture in a nationwide net-work of good old boys, cohorts to whom each could turn for aid and assistance.

So, I did what I had done several times in the past. I called Ben.

He groaned at my lack of evidence; warned me of the risk of tangling with Mississippi law; provided me a name; and swore he would not post my bail when they slammed my worthless carcass behind bars.

I chuckled. "Why don't you tell me what you really think, Ben?"

He called me a couple of names I would never say around my mother. One thing about him however, he knew the important people. And he did not hesitate to send me to the one who could help most, Vicksburg's finest, Chief of Police Field Hemings.

The name, Hemings, still hadn't registered when I was shown to the office of the police chief. I opened the door and saw a lanky black man in khaki pants and shirt with a black tie squatting by a battered desk. He was picking up pieces of glass off the floor and dropping them in the trashcan.

The janitor, I figured. I glanced about the room, searching for the chief.

Casually, he drawled in a deep voice, "Who are you looking for, boy?"

Boy? Boy? And then for some inexplicable reason, I felt intimidated. Clearing my throat nervously, I replied, "I'm looking for Chief Hemings."

With a slight nod, he rose to his feet and looking down at me, replied, "You found him."

And then the name, Hemings, registered.

Unable to hide my surprise or suppress the shock of the sudden realization that I was face to face with a purported descendent of President Thomas Jefferson, I just stared at Chief Hemings while the controversial story of Jefferson and Sally Hemings flashed through my mind.

He arched an eyebrow and a slow grin spread over his face. "You wouldn't happen to be that little Cajun boy from Church Point, Louisiana, would you?"

"H–how did you know?"

He gestured to a captain's chair in front of his worn oak desk. "Well, boy, Ben told me about you." He shook his head as he plopped down in his wooden swivel chair, which squeaked under his weight. "He said you were sticking your nose in something that maybe you shouldn't." He paused and leaned back. Still smiling amicably, he added, "I don't cotton to outsiders who cause me problems or interfere with my business." He was still smiling.

My ears burned.

Before I could reply, he continued, "But I've known Ben for a long time. That's why I'm talking to you on this side of jailhouse bars instead of through them."

I relaxed, but despite the smile on his face, I realized that Field Hemings could be a formidable opponent if he chose. And I certainly did not want him to choose. "And that's exactly why I called Ben and came to see you, Chief. I'm licensed in Texas, but not here. I don't want to create any problems." I paused for his response.

He pursed his lips for several seconds before nodding for me to continue.

At least he hadn't thrown me out. Quickly, I laid out Jack's suspicion, his subsequent hiring of me, the cement bag that barely missed me, the erroneous conclusion as to the source of the fire, and the bitter contention among the family regarding the will.

When I finished, he studied me a moment. "Well, boy, Ben was right. You don't have much to work with. It all could be marked off as coincidence."

"I know. That's why I want your permission to see the fire marshal's report and the autopsy results when they are available. Jack can get me a copy of the will. Whatever I find, one way or another, you get first. And at the same time, I'm satisfying my client."

For what seemed like hours, Chief Hemings stared at me, pondering my request. "Like I said," he growled, "I got me a good town here, and I won't tolerate no trouble." His eyes narrowed as he leaned forward and punched a button on the intercom. "Jimmy, send Garrett in here." He punched off. His eyes narrowed. "Because Ben asked, I'll give you a hand. Tom Garrett is your contact. He'll get you copies of the fire marshal's report and the autopsy. You'll give him every scrap of whatever you find. Understood?"

"You mean the autopsy is complete?"

"We don't waste time around here, boy."

"Thanks," I said as the door opened, and Tom Garrett entered. Under a rumpled tan blazer, he wore a blue denim shirt unbuttoned at the collar and washed-out jeans. He was a couple of inches taller than me at about six feet or so, and weighed about one-ninety, ten of which probably came from the bushiest eyebrows I'd ever seen. He shot me an indifferent glance. "What's up, Chief?"

The chief introduced me and briefly explained what I was after. "You're his contact."

Garrett rolled his eyes. "Come on, Chief. I got cases to work on without wasting time with some nosy PI. Give it to someone else."

Hemings' eyes grew cold. In a flat voice, he said, "You're it, Garrett. Get it done."

Garrett stared at Hemings for several seconds. I could feel the electricity crackling in the air, and I quickly came to the conclusion there was no love lost between the two.

Being a southern boy, I didn't have to wonder why. As much as I detested it, there were still pockets of prejudice in our part of the country. Fortunately, those cubicles of hate were growing both smaller and fewer. I was lucky growing up. We were not subjected to extreme prejudice in my hometown for the races lived shoulder to shoulder. My best friend and boyhood chum was Leroi Thibodeaux, who not only was black, but also my cousin.

Finally, Garrett dropped his eyes and shook his head. "Whatever you say, Chief Hemings," he said, emphasizing the chief's title. He cut his eyes at me. "Let's go." Without another word, he spun on his heel and stomped from the office.

"Thanks, Chief," I said, standing and extending my hand. "I promise. No trouble." And I meant it, but it turned out to be one of those promises impossible to keep.

"And Boudreaux?"

"Yeah?"

"You carry a piece?"

I nodded. "A .38. I got a license."

He grinned crookedly. "For Texas."

With a sheepish smile, I replied, "For Texas."

For a moment, he studied me. "Lock it in your glove compartment until you leave, or you'll have the doubtful privilege of enjoying the hospitality of our jail."

"Whatever you say, Chief."

Garrett plopped down at his desk and grabbed the phone, completely ignoring my presence, so I followed his lead and plopped down in the chair beside his desk. Though irritated by his rude manners, I remained silent. All I wanted was the autopsy and fire marshal's report in my hot little hand. I could put up with any cretin until then.

I looked around. Several desks were arranged in rows throughout the room, a couple of which were occupied by other detectives who stared with unabashed curiosity at me.

Garrett barked orders over the phone, then slammed it down. He glared at me, his bushy eyebrows meeting over the bridge of his nose. "This is a waste of time, Boudreaux. I hope you know that."

Up until that point, I had no particular personal feelings one way or another about Tom Garrett, but now, I was beginning to truly dislike the man. "Then I suggest we get it done as fast as we can. You point me where I can pick up those reports, and I'll get out of here."

For a moment, he didn't reply. Finally he shook his head. "Hemings said I was your contact. Just you sit there and wait."

Under my breath, I called Jack Edney every name in the book. Twelve hundred bucks a day wasn't half enough to have to tolerate a bad-mannered jerk like Tom Garrett. I pushed myself to my feet. "Why wait? Let's get the reports."

A smug grin curled his lips, and he leaned back in his chair. He pointed to the fax machine across the squad room. "We ain't going nowhere, Country Boy. It's coming to us. Or don't they have faxes where you come from down in Podunk Holler?"

One of the other detectives snickered.

I almost snapped, but I maintained my composure. "Yeah.

We have faxes, and we also have meatballs like you, and from time to time, I have to kick their tails up between their shoulders just to remind them of their place."

His face darkened, and he started to rise.

In a soft, cold voice, I warned him. "I don't know if you're always this stupid or you're just making a special effort for me, Garrett, but getting out of that chair could be one of the dumbest things you have ever done." I knotted my fists, praying Garrett would stand up.

He hesitated halfway up, his eyes on mine, measuring my resolution. I guess he didn't like what he saw because he gave a feeble laugh and dropped back into his chair.

I remained standing. Behind me, the snickering ceased. At that moment, the fax machine whirred. Without a word, I crossed the room and pulled out the reports, and all the while, I could feel his eyes burning holes in my back.

Pausing at a vacant desk, I stapled the reports and held them up for Garrett to see. "I'll stay in touch," I said, heading for the door, my blood pressure just below meltdown.

Chapter Six

W hen Annebelle Edney slipped into her plastic raincoat around 6:30, two or three minutes after her brothers had left for the memorial service, I grinned to myself. I figured she was deliberately hanging back so she wouldn't have to ride with them. And I didn't blame her although from what I had witnessed, she deserved as much blame for their disagreements as Stewart or WR.

Outside, the drizzle turned into a downpour, slamming against the old house with a deafening roar. I decided to use my time alone to go over the autopsy, the fire marshal's report, and a copy of the will Jack had given me.

The medical examiner's report was unremarkable. Physically, the old man was in good shape. He died by asphyxiation as a result of smoke inhalation. In addition to the body having been partially consumed by the fire, the medical examiner reported a blunt trauma to the occipital region. In fact the way the report read was *after transflecting the scalp, a blunt trauma force to the left temporal area of the cranium was located.*

I didn't know exactly what all of it meant, so I prowled the house for a dictionary. I shook my head in wonder at medical jargon. "Why couldn't they just say that they removed the scalp and his left temple was smashed in," I muttered, closing the dictionary.

The ME further concluded that the injury was sustained when Edney fell from the explosion, slamming his head against the concrete floor of the garage.

At that moment, I didn't figure what little information I picked up from the report was worth the trouble I went through with Tom Garrett to get it.

The credibility of the fire marshal's report was suspect as far as I was concerned because it stated unequivocally the spark that ignited the naphtha occurred when Edney was cleaning the brass fireplace tools, an impossible chemical reaction between naphtha and any soft metal, one as unlikely to occur as my old man to quit drinking.

With a sigh, I turned to the will, which was only a few pages. It simply listed several generous bequests to various organizations, both civic and fraternal, as well as a $10,000 bequest to Alice Windsor, his housekeeper. Once all the bequests were made, then the four heirs would share all property equally.

My first question was what property?

Back in Austin, the top sleuth in our agency was Al Grogan. I was nowhere near his class, but I had learned much from him, primarily how to think logically. Believe me, for someone with my background in rural Louisiana who grew up believing that it always rained when a pig squealed, acquiring the capability of logical reasoning was a major chore.

I knew that before any will could be probated, there must be an inventory of properties. Since I had the gut feeling that Edney's death was not an accident, maybe I could find a hint of motive in the inventory.

I thumbed through the folder of documents Jack had given me. "Well, well," I muttered, discovering several pages stapled together. At the top of the first page was 'Property Inventory.'

I whistled as I read down the inventory list. John Wesley Edney was indeed well off. His physical property in town, the homestead and various buildings that he leased out, exceeded an estimated $4 million. Financial assets were another $4 million. Then I found the land south of town Annebelle and WR had discussed. It was a thousand and ten acres of riverside property twenty miles below Vicksburg. WR had claimed it was worthless. I was curious as to what he considered worthless.

So, I did what any red-blooded American boy would do. I picked up the telephone, called a real estate agent at his after-hours number, and started lying.

"Yeah, partner," I said, exaggerating a Texas drawl. "I know it's past closing time, but I just drove into town from Fort Worth. I'll be here a couple days, looking for riverside property ten or fifteen miles below Vicksburg. Something reasonable for my thoroughbred horses."

The agent on the other end of the line chuckled. Amiably, he replied. "Sorry, Tex, but there's nothing reasonable down there. Hasn't been for the last couple years."

Since my whole story was a fabrication, I decided to play the role to the hilt. "Well, maybe I should explain what I mean by reasonable. My oil and gas wells have been pumping mighty good, so good I'd be willing to go three, maybe even four thousand an acre."

He laughed. "Sorry again, friend. Kick it up to ten or twelve and throw in one or two of those wells, and maybe you could pick up a couple acres." He grew serious. "Truth is, ever since word got out that the government is planning to build a new north-south interstate from Lafayette, Louisiana, to Vicksburg, property along the way has been hotter than a blowtorch in Hades."

I expressed my disappointment, thanked him, hung up, and shook my head in wonder. Over a thousand acres at twelve thousand each. Jeez. Unless my math was off, we were talking about a nice little nest egg of $12 million.

Add the other assets, and the old man's estate could total as much as twenty million, give or take a nickel or so.

Regardless of the nickel, that was more than enough money to drive even emotionally stable families to desperate steps. And when I considered just how dysfunctional the Edney clan was, I couldn't even imagine the limits to which one or all of the siblings might go, maybe with the exception of Jack. But then, money can wreak unexpected changes in the best of people.

After first grasping at straws, I now found myself with a haystack full of motives, twenty million of them to be exact.

For several moments, I considered where to start. I glanced out the window. The downpour had subsided into a fine mist.

I closed my eyes for a moment. I didn't realize just how tired I was. I must have dozed, for my head jerked back sharply, awakening me. "Jeez," I muttered. "What a day." I shook myself awake and, sticking the folder of documents under my jacket, grabbed an umbrella, and headed out to the burned shop, detouring by way of my pickup for a flashlight. When in doubt, I told myself, begin at the beginning.

The rain and drizzle had erased most of the marks made by the criminalists investigating the scene. Their notes were as detailed as possible given the fact the fire had obliterated much of the evidence that might have been helpful.

Huddling under my umbrella and shining the beam along the ground, I paused by the charred wood table where the fire began. Despite the sodden ashes melting into unrecognizable shapes and heaps, I saw nothing on or around the timbered workbench that could have been the source of the spark.

The only tools that could have ignited the cleaning fluid were buried under the ashes along the outside wall where they had been hanging, fifteen feet from where the fire began, much too far to create a spark.

The steady drizzle had washed away most of the lines the

criminalists had drawn on the concrete floor indicating the position of the body. From what I could ascertain, Edney's body was discovered at the base of the table. Time of death was put at 2:40 on the afternoon of the twenty-sixth, the time his watch stopped.

I tried to put myself in the scene. I'm cleaning fireplace tools. The naphtha ignites; my clothes catch fire. So what do I do? What would anyone do? Fall on the floor at the base of the table?

Not quite.

I'd run like wild hogs were after me. Anyone would.

The drizzle came down harder. I hurried next door to the garage housing the restored vehicles.

Once inside, I leaned the umbrella against the wall to drain. The rain kept up a steady patter on the metal roof, like the soft thrumming of drums.

I stared at the rows of shiny automobiles under the bright lights, then headed directly for the Model T Runabout. Opening the door, I climbed in, admiring the immaculate interior. Not a bad little car, I told myself, feeling the first hint of car fever.

Glancing at the passenger's side, for a fleeting moment I imagined Janice on the seat. "She'd probably get a kick out of a spin in this little car," I muttered. One thing in her favor, she never turned down the opportunity to try something new, something different.

Leaning back on the seat, I pulled out the criminalists' report again. Included were the pictures of the scene. I grimaced when I saw the charred lump purported to be John Wesley Edney at the base of the table.

Since the picture was a facsimile, the definition was blurred. I angled it so the light would shine on it directly. I struggled to make out the corpse's limbs, but the fire had practically consumed him. Still, I could make out where one arm ended. As the ME's report stated, the corpse lay on his right side in a fetal position facing the table.

My eyes narrowed. All killers make mistakes. And this one had made a second mistake. But, even with the non-sparking brass, this second error was not enough to lead me to his identity, but it convinced me the fire was no accident.

John Wesley Edney had been struck in the left temple, and the fire intentionally set to make it appear an accident.

I visualized the scene in my head. The old man was facing the table. His assailant struck from behind, and for the wound to be on the left temple, the killer was probably left-handed.

Not that I ruled out right-handers. One could have initiated the swing backhanded, but unless he used both hands, the force would not be enough to render JW Edney unconscious long enough to suffocate.

To me, my theory made sense. If he were struck from behind on the left temple, he would have fallen to his right, facing the table. Exactly where the body had been found.

A nagging feeling came over me. Something didn't fit. I pulled out the ME's report and read once again that the body had been discovered lying in a fetal position on its right side.

I glanced at the autopsy results once again, which concluded the head injury was sustained when Edney fell from the explosion, slamming his head against the concrete.

For several moments, I studied the report. If I were to believe the autopsy report, then why was the injury on the left side instead of the right?

I shook my head. That didn't make sense. Someone had murdered JW Edney.

I pulled out my cell phone.

Now was the time to put in a call to my savior on more than one occasion, Eddie Dyson—computer whiz, entrepreneur, and at one time, Austin's resident sleazy-bar stool pigeon.

A few years earlier, Eddie gave up the uncertain life of a snitch working squalid bars for the snug comfort of computers and credit cards. He had pulled onto the fast lane of the information superhighway and had quickly become a successful driver on the road.

Any information I couldn't find, he could. There were

only two catches if you dealt with Eddie. First, you never asked him how he found the information, and second, he only accepted Visa credit cards for payment.

Sometimes his charges were expensive, sometimes reasonable, never cheap. But, failure was not in his vocabulary.

And failure was the last thing I needed now.

In the morning, I told myself, as much as I disliked the man, I had to enlist Tom Garrett's assistance in getting me in to visit with the medical examiner.

Chapter Seven

As I completed my transaction with Eddie, headlights flashed through the rain-drenched window. I rolled my eyes, not relishing being around the squabbling family this evening.

Deliberately, I remained in the garage.

A few minutes later, Jack showed up, a raincoat draped over his cast and a wry scowl on his face.

I nodded to him. "How was the memorial service?"

"No problem. We had to wait for Annebelle. She was supposed to be right behind us, but as usual, she fiddled around and showed up ten or fifteen minutes late. At least, no one got into a fight. By the way, what happened to your truck?"

"My truck? Nothing. Why?"

"Nothing?" He grunted. "You got a strange idea of nothing, pal." He headed for the door. "You better come take a look."

A brick had been thrown through the window on the passenger's side. It lay on the floorboard surrounded by slivers of glass. On the seat, neatly placed on top of the shattered glass, was a sheet of paper.

Cursing to myself, I jerked open the door and grabbed the paper.

Keep your nose out of business that don't concern you.
Last warning.

"What does it say?"

Without a word, I handed it to him. The hackles on the back of my neck rose. The bag of cement earlier in the day had been no accident.

Jack whistled and handed me the note. "What's going on?"

I ignored his question. "Have you told anyone about me?"

"About my suspicions? No."

"What about earlier when I went down to the parts house?"

He nodded, frowning. "Yeah. Just after you left, I was headed for the john when WR asked where you were going. I told them. Stewart asked what kind of business you were in, so I told them."

"That I was a PI?"

"Yeah. Was that wrong?"

I shook my head. "Well, it's too late to worry about it now. How long were you gone, to the john, I mean?"

He glanced sidelong at his cast. "Five, maybe ten minutes. With this thing, it takes time. You ever try buttoning your pants with one hand?"

"Not lately," I replied, considering his words. If one of them had called as soon as Jack left the room, the construction worker would have had twenty, maybe twenty-five minutes to get into position to drop the cement.

Jack spoke up. "You don't think one of them was behind it, do you, Tony?"

I shrugged off his question, but I told myself it could be any of the three, or all.

A gust of wind swept the drizzle under the umbrella. I grimaced. "I'm going to pull the truck in the garage so I can patch the window."

Jack stared at the shattered window. "How are you going to do that?"

"Tape some plastic over it."

"Tape?"

I climbed in the truck and grinned at him. "Duct tape." I hooked my thumb to the toolbox in back. "Always carry it, and WD-Forty." From the dome light, I saw the puzzlement scribbled across his face. "WD-Forty for the things that are supposed to move, but don't, and duct tape for the things that are not supposed to move, but do. Cajun's toolbox."

Fifteen minutes later, I had a patch on the window and the glass brushed from the truck. "Well, not as good as new, but it'll work until I get another one in tomorrow."

"Okay. If you're finished, let's go up to the house. WR is calling in some pizza."

I declined. "I've got some thinking to do. I'll find me a steakhouse around somewhere, then get me a motel." I glanced at the house and shook my head.

"I'll go with you."

"No. I told you, I've got some thinking to do."

"About my old man?"

"About a lot of things, Jack. For example, did you know your father had riverside property down below Vicksburg?"

His forehead wrinkled in concentration. "Yeah. Some swampland not worth a plugged nickel from what WR said."

I decided against telling him the truth at that moment. The less he knew, the better off I was with the investigation. There was no question in my cynical mind that the other three siblings already knew the property was far from worthless.

Jack waved from the front porch as I drove away.

I glanced in the rearview as I drove away, and with a mixed sense of relief and guilt, spotted his rotund silhouette standing forlornly under the hazy glare of the porch light. I don't know why, I just did. Maybe it was because I hated to leave him behind with those three vultures. For all Jack's misadventures, he was basically a harmless guy.

My tires hissed on the wet streets as I headed back toward Washington. I'd noticed a motel, the Riverside Inn, on the levee.

It was reasonably priced and clean with cable and the other amenities. My eyes were drooping, and my stomach was growling. I eyed the bed hungrily, but my rumbling stomach won out. Across the street was Casper's Steak and Shrimp House. I dashed across the busy street to the restaurant and slipped into a booth near a window so I could watch the passing cars in the rain.

"Yes, sir," a bubbly voice said as a hand slipped the menu in front of me.

I glanced up and froze.

Staring down at me with an equally surprised look on her face was my ex-wife, Diane Mays.

For several seconds, we just stared at each other before I jumped to my feet. "Diane." We were both too flustered to speak. Instinctively, we just hugged each other before awkwardly pushing away. "Well, how are you?" I managed to stammer out.

Nearby patrons stared at us curiously.

Blushing, she glanced at them, at the same time pushing her hair back from her forehead. "Fine. I'm fine. I, ah . . ."

Suddenly, we both broke into laughter. I looked around at the onlookers and threw out my arms. "Sorry, folks. We, ah, well, we were once married, but we haven't seen each other in years."

From a nearby table, a man quipped, "That must be the secret of staying friends." He laughed, and his wife glared daggers at him. Looked like someone was in for a chilly night.

Finally, we managed to get my order in and arranged to meet next door in the bar after the restaurant closed at midnight.

I couldn't help watching her throughout the meal, and she must have felt the same, for she kept glancing at me with a big smile. I remembered that smile the first time I saw it back in high school. She was attractive then, and attractive now. Her shiny brown hair and flashing black eyes brought back the days when those features played flip-flop with my heart.

After paying the bill and leaving her a generous tip, I reminded her of our date.

"I won't forget," she replied with a coquettish smile on her lips.

Back in my room, I flipped on the TV and plopped down on the bed, wide awake. I opened the visitors' brochure on the Vicksburg Battlefield and skimmed over the sixteen-mile route and the various sites along the way, but Diane was too much on my mind.

She and I were high school sweethearts in Church Point. We started college together, but she dropped out, and we drifted apart. Several years later, we got back together, legally.

Unlike most of our friends who made one baby after another because they believed God had placed them on earth to procreate the entire world all by themselves, Diane and I had no offspring, and within two years, the thrill of lust and passion quickly faded when we woke each morning and faced each other at our worst.

Somewhere along the way, something died between us. I'm not smart enough to know what. I wish I did. Maybe that was the same problem now facing Janice and me.

All I can say about our divorce is that we parted amicably. Diane took her clothes, the furniture, the car, and I took my clothes, a ten-gallon aquarium with Oscar, his swimming mates, and a taxi cab. Like the words in an old country song from way back, "She Got the Gold Mine, and I Got the Shaft." But I never regretted the split at all. I was satisfied with Oscar, a tiny Albino Tiger Barb, and his cohorts, a few Tiger and Checker Barbs.

Once I put some Angelfish in with the Barbs, but the little Barbs chased the docile little Angels around the aquarium, nipping at their fins. The Angels would probably have died with heart attacks if Jack Edney hadn't come along.

On a drunken spree, he urinated in the aquarium thinking,

well, I don't know what he was thinking. Next morning, all the little exotics except Oscar were floating belly up, and Oscar just swam in circles. Some kind of brain damage, I surmised.

Naturally, Jack, like all murderers, showed great remorse and regret when he sobered up, but the damage was done.

In the bar, Diane and I took a table near the dance floor. Diane ordered a draft beer, and I ordered a Coca-Cola. When she arched an inquisitive eyebrow, I explained. "AA. Three years now."

She nodded. "My beer going to bother you?"

I grinned mischievously. "It'll drive me crazy, but I can manage." I laughed and shook my head. "Don't worry about it. It won't bother me." That was a tiny lie. It did bother me, and that was one of the reasons I did not frequent bars any longer. But tonight was an exception. I could handle one evening of temptation, I hoped.

As we reminisced, I told myself she hadn't changed much. Oh, her skin wasn't as tight as it had been, but then, whose is once you get into the late thirties? Despite my random exercises, I was sagging in more places than I cared to admit.

At least, we hadn't reached the point in life that even if we did throw caution to the wind and let it all hang out no one would pay any attention.

After our divorce, Diane moved to Houston, married, divorced, moved back to Church Point, and finally landed a job at the Vicksburg National Battlefield with the National Park Service.

The job at the steakhouse was part-time, helping out her friend, Jaybird, who owned the restaurant. "Besides," she said with a sly grin, "the tips are fantastic." She lowered her voice and glanced around. "And you don't have to report them."

I brought her up to date with me.

"So, you drove your friend over here for his father's funeral?"

"Yep. Jack Edney. You didn't know him. After we broke up, I moved to an apartment complex on Travis Street. He and his wife moved in later."

I thought I saw a flicker of surprise in her eyes, but I passed it off as the reflection of the jukebox from the other side of the dance floor.

As I walked her to her car later, I suggested getting together the next night.

Diane hesitated. "Well, I had plans, but—" A broad smile played over her lips. "I enjoyed tonight, Tony. And it has been a long time. Give me a call. I'll see what I can work out."

I dreamed of Diane that night and woke next morning with the feeling I had betrayed Janice.

Chapter Eight

Next morning, I called Tom Garrett at the police station to inform him of the brick that had been tossed through my window and the note left on the seat.

"Too bad," he said with a chuckle. "For your information, Chief Hemings told me why he was giving you some freedom around here. Personally, I don't care what he owes anybody—just don't you do nothing that'll put you crossways with me. I don't like playing nursemaid to nobody."

I didn't argue with the man. I just didn't want to give him the opportunity to claim I had not kept in touch with him. "Well, I was going to ask you to set up a time I could visit with the medical examiner. But, if it's going to be a pain, I'll take care of it myself. I can get his name from the chief." I paused. "Actually, I think I'd prefer that."

He hesitated. He was probably debating Hemings' reaction to whichever decision he made. He muttered a curse. "Give me a telephone number. I'll call the ME and have him get in touch with you."

The suggestion did not appeal to me. On the other hand, maybe the jerk would follow through just to keep Hemings off his back. "All right, but I need to talk this morning."

Testily, he shot back, "All right, all right. What's the number?"

I gave him Jack's number, thanked him, and hung up before he could reply.

Jack was the only one at the house. Annebelle was on her bread run; Stewart was curling hair at his hair salon; and WR was at his hardware store.

"You've got to stay here with me, Tony," Jack said over a cup of coffee, which he abruptly sat down, and grabbed for the emu feather. He frantically went to work on his arm. "This house is too big for one man," he added, grimacing. "Man, this itching is driving me nuts."

I had spotted an elderly housekeeper when I came in. "What about domestic help?"

"Day help." With teeth clenched against the itch, he nodded to the kitchen. "That's Alice. She's been with John for years. Comes in about seven, leaves around three or four. That's how John wanted it."

"What about his supper?"

He lifted an eyebrow. "John never ate supper."

Whatever, I thought. Eyeing the elaborately engraved cornice molding in the high-ceiling room in which we sat, I asked, "What about your brothers and sister?"

Still pumping away with the feather, he muttered, "They got their own places. We're all getting together this afternoon to divide the property."

"Wasting no time, huh?"

Jack shrugged. "As I understand the process, probate takes some time. If we can settle all our differences and make our decisions early, the probate will go faster." Finally, he stopped scratching and, leaving the emu feather projecting from his cast, took another sip of his coffee. "What about you? Come up with any ideas last night?"

"Nope. Drew a blank," I replied, deliberately not mentioning my date with Diane. "Figured I'd hit the ground running this morning. First, I'd like to prowl through your father's records."

"Sure. No problem. What are you looking for?"

"The reason someone wants to run me off."

At that moment, the phone rang. Jack answered, then handed it to me.

"Mr. Boudreaux. This is Dr. John Samson. Detective Garrett of the Vicksburg Police Department said you wanted to talk to me about the autopsy of John Wesley Edney." The caution in his tone was unmistakable.

Long ago, I learned when interviewing never to blame anyone except myself for mistakes. The technique is a sneaky, but effective method to elicit aid and information. "I probably read the report wrong, Doctor, but I was curious. The injury was on the left temple. I interpreted the report to indicate the wound was caused when Mr. Edney fell, but the report also states he was found lying on his right side. If that's the case, how could a blow from falling on the right side cause an injury on the left? Or am I confused?"

He cleared his throat. "I'm looking at the report now," he finally said, his words tentative. "Oh, yes. Indications were that Mr. Edney turned around to escape the fire, putting the table at his back, then stumbled and fell to his left, causing the trauma. The blow stunned him. He never regained consciousness. He was asphyxiated by the fumes, then consumed by the fire."

"But, how did he get on his right side?"

With a trace of disdain in his tone, he replied, "Obviously, he turned over as a result of his struggles during the throes of asphyxiation. Conjecture of course, but given lack of further evidence, our final conclusion."

If I hadn't known better, I would have thought I was listening to an old Three Stooges dialogue. "Facing the work bench?"

"Correct." He paused. I could hear the anxiety in his voice. "Was that all you needed?"

A wry grin curled my lips. Any further information I elicited from this one wouldn't be worth the time. "Yeah, Doc. That's it. Thanks for making it perfectly clear to me."

"Anytime."

I replaced the receiver and leaned back in the wingback chair. I looked at Jack. "Medical examiner."

Jack paused in stroking his feather. "Find out anything?"

Pursing my lips, I studied him. "Nothing, other than that gentleman had better never go into private practice. He'll end up neck deep in malpractice suits. Now, where did your father keep his records?"

A frown creased Jack's forehead. "You think the medical examiner is involved?"

"No." I laughed. "I think he's merely an incompetent who got the job either because his brother is the mayor, or somebody had something on someone."

For the next two hours and two pots of coffee, all I discovered about John Wesley Edney was that he was a well-organized man. Unfortunately, there was no smoking gun—at least not one I could see. I frowned when I ran across a puzzling sheath of letters to various individuals and businesses confirming previous commitments. Then I discovered a map of the thousand and ten acres south of Vicksburg. I decided to take a look at the property when I finished going through his files.

Over the years, Edney had loaned both WR and Stewart money on several occasions. The loans were the sort parents make to offspring knowing full well they'll never be paid back.

The amounts loaned out varied. Both WR and Stewart were into their father for a few hundred thousand. As I would have expected, neither Annebelle nor Jack had received a nickel.

Any time I worked a case, I tried to come up with an arbitrary suspect. If it appeared the perpetrator was a professional, then I would turn to the records of those professionals possessing that particular modus operandi, and establish their current whereabouts so I could determine if any of them had the opportunity.

If it did not appear to be a professional job, then I figured it was the result of passion, one carried out because the opportunity presented itself. That being the case, then I looked for motives such as anger, profit, revenge, and any other of a number of reasons.

I already had three suspects. Now, it was just a matter of legwork and digging deep into everyone's business.

Chapter Nine

J ack rushed in just before lunch, a look of panic on his face. "Tony, you got to help me." He paused with only half a feather in his hand.

"What's going on?"

He pointed the broken feather at his cast. "It broke. The stinking feather broke inside the cast, and I can't get it out. All those little feathers in there are driving me crazy."

I burst out laughing.

"It isn't funny. I can't stand it, I tell you. It feels like a bunch of cockroaches crawling over my skin."

Tears rolled down my cheeks. I shook my head. "Sorry, Jack. I can't help it. It's just . . ." Another burst of laughter cut off my words.

"You got to call a doctor or emergency room or something, Tony. Maybe they can blow something up there."

Suppressing my laughter, I managed to stammer out, "All right, all right. In the meantime, find some talcum powder and sprinkle it down the cast. Maybe that'll help."

He nodded emphatically. "That might work. You know, that might just work," he muttered between clenched teeth as he hurried from the room.

A couple of minutes later, the phone rang. I answered. It

was Doc Raines. He wanted to talk to Jack or one of the kids. "Jack'll be right back. The others aren't here. Can I help?"

"I just wanted to let them know I have a couple guys interested in some of JW's cars."

"I'll pass that along, Doc. By the way, when we first talked, you said Stewart ordered the naphtha."

"That's right."

"How do you know it was him?"

Doc chuckled. "That high-pitched voice? No way it wasn't. I could pick him out of a thousand voices."

"I see. Changing the subject, I've been thinking about that Model T Runabout. I'd have to find somewhere to store it, but I might be real interested in it. You think fifteen thousand is a fair price?"

"Fair enough. Like I said, there's gas tank problems. You'd have to repair it or put a new one in. And when I got to thinking about it after you left, JW also had a problem with the wiper arm."

At that moment, Jack came back into the room. I blinked. His face and chest were covered with talcum powder. He looked like a circus clown in white face, his cast at half-mast.

He mouthed "Who?"

Pointing to the receiver, I mouthed "Doc."

Jack grinned and nodded at the receiver. "The Doc?"

I nodded. "All right, Doc," I said. "I have a pencil and paper. Tell me how to go about taking care of it."

Jack grinned and pointed to his cast. "About the cast?"

Too preoccupied with the details of the gas tank, I nodded and waved him off, having not the slightest idea that at that moment he believed I was talking about him.

"You're not thinking about doing it yourself, are you?" Skepticism laced Doc's question.

I forgot about Jack for the moment. "Sure, Doc. I can do it myself. Shouldn't be a problem. The arm too. Now, shoot."

Jack nodded, pointing to himself and then to me. A grimace screwed up his face, and he beat on his cast. "Hurry up," he gasped. "This is killing me. This talcum powder doesn't work. I had to lay on my back and pour it down the cast. That's how I got it all over me."

Quickly I jotted down the steps in replacing the gas tank and wiper arm. "I got it, Doc. And thanks." I winked at Jack. "I'm sure Jack appreciates your help. What's that? Oh, the arm. Yeah, I understand. We'll see." I replaced the receiver.

Jack nodded to the slip of paper in my hand. "What did the Doc say? What did he say?"

For a moment, I wondered why Jack was so interested in replacing a gas tank on the Runabout, but I dismissed the thought.

"Doc said the problem was caused by trash inside. It needs to come out. He said by now the trash probably looks like a bunch of rotted leaves."

"Rotted leaves?" Jack curled his lips in distaste and gave his cast a puzzled look. He rubbed at the cast. "That's what's causing the problem?"

"Well, part of it."

"So, what's the rest?"

I frowned at him, baffled over his preoccupation with the gas tank. With a shrug, I read from the notes in my hand to humor him. "There are two or three options. First, we can go down to his place and get some stuff to slush around inside. That might stop it."

Jack shot a horrified look at his cast. "Slush around inside? But, won't it melt?"

"Melt? Of course not."

He frowned at his cast. "I don't like the idea of pouring something inside and slushing it around. You said he had a couple options. What's the other?"

"Well, it's drastic, but I could cut it in two lengthwise. That way I can get to it without a problem."

Jack's face paled. He took a hasty step backward and placed his right arm over his cast protectively. "No way. No cutting. Absolutely not."

I was truly puzzled now. I had no idea he had become

attached so quickly to his father's restorations. With a sigh, I shook my head. "Those are the cheap ways to go. The best costs more."

"I don't know about you, old friend," he said, sarcasm oozing from his words as he glanced at his cast, "but I'd pay whatever is necessary to keep it."

"Yeah, but it's extreme, although it's probably the best way."

"So? What is it? It has to be better than either of those first two remedies."

"Well, the best solution is simply to yank it off the body and replace it with a new one."

Jack gaped at me. "You've got to be kidding."

I just stared at him. "No."

His voice filled with disbelief, he stammered. "Th—the arm?"

He had me confused now. "Yeah. The arm. He said the new ones made out of plastic would last a lifetime."

Eyes wide, Jack backed away. "You're not cutting off my arm or slushing anything around in the cast. No way."

I had the feeling I'd just stepped into the old "Twilight Zone." Then it hit me. "You mean—" I pointed to the receiver. "You thought that—" I couldn't finish my question because I was laughing so hard.

Poor Jack, he just stood there with a puzzled and confused expression on his face. When I managed to catch my breath, I explained that I was not talking to a medical doctor, but to Doc Raines about the gas tank and wiper arm on the Model T Runabout.

"And not my arm?"

"No, Jack. Not your arm."

With an embarrassed grin, he sighed, then grimaced. "I gotta find something to stop this blasted itching." He turned on his heel. "I'll be right back."

Jack returned moments later with a fly swatter sticking out of his cast. "It's better than nothing," he said, busily sliding it in and out.

Nodding to a nearby chair, I said, "We need to talk."

He plopped down. "Make it fast. My arm's driving me nuts."

Despite the complaining I've done about him, Jack was a good friend, and I was reluctant to upset him, but if I was to continue my investigation, I had to be honest with him. "Jack. I've something to tell you. After you hear what I have to say, you decide if you want me to continue the investigation or not."

He frowned, puzzled. "I don't follow you."

I took a deep breath. "It could very well be that one, maybe all of your brothers and your sister are responsible for the death of your father."

He grimaced as if I'd kicked him in the stomach. "Are–are you sure?"

"No. I'm not sure of anything, but it appears that's the direction we're heading."

"Did you find anything in John's files that makes you think that?" He gestured to the file cabinet.

"Not much other than he loaned WR and Stewart a lot of money they never paid back."

Jack chuckled. "Now why doesn't that surprise me?" He paused. "Do you think you can find any evidence that will tell you who killed John?"

"There's always evidence. The trick is not only finding it, but then also interpreting it correctly." I nodded. "It's there. It'll just take time to uncover it. I'm telling you all of this because it's time your family knows what I'm doing."

"They'll be mad knowing you suspect them."

"They can take it up with the police chief. He gave me his blessing to investigate your father's death." I paused. "Well?"

"Well what?"

"Do I go on? It's up to you, Jack. If you want to drop it now, just say so." I had mixed feelings. I hated to see deliberate injury against another go unpunished, yet if my suspicions proved true, Jack would be hurt. Conscience or friendship. Heck of a choice. I knew what I would do, but I left the final decision up to Jack.

He chewed on his bottom lip, then nodded firmly. "If someone killed John, I want to know who it was. But I can't believe it was one of us."

The grandfather clock struck 11.

Jack jumped. "Hey, Tony, about tonight. You are staying here aren't you?"

I started to refuse, but the pleading look on his face got the better of me. Reluctantly I caved in. "I suppose."

He grinned in relief. "Then you better check out of the motel before they charge you for another day." He nodded to his cast. "And look, see if you can find me another feather. I've got to have something. This fly swatter is rubbing me raw."

Chapter Ten

Before I returned with my gear to the old house, I took a run south of town. Twenty miles down, after inquiring at a Mom and Pop convenience store, I found the property, and to my surprise, a realtor's sign prominently on display. I read it aloud. "Bayou Realtors, Vicksburg." In the lower corner was the realtor's designation, "Property #38." Pulling to the side of the highway, I jotted the telephone number as well as the property number. This was one real estate agent I wanted to visit.

On the way back to Vicksburg, I called Bayou Realtors for directions to their office.

A white-brick building with picture windows spanning the front housed Bayou Realtors. The neat office sat on a well-manicured lot adjacent to the Vicksburg Battlefield. A Ford Taurus was parked in front.

For several moments, I studied the building. Someone didn't want me snooping. He, or she, had made that abundantly clear. As far as I knew, the realtor might be part of whatever was going on. Just to play safe, I decided to be an out-of-town land speculator searching for cheap land to develop.

* * *

Inside, the young woman behind the receptionist's desk looked up and smiled warmly. "Yes, sir, can I help you?"

"I hope so," I said, falling into the pretext role of a prospective buyer. "I was curious about a piece of land south of town, Property Thirty-Eight. It could fit the bill for some developments I'm working on. What's the asking price on it?"

She turned to her computer on her right, input the information, then nodded when it flashed on the screen. "That piece consists of one thousand and ten acres."

I could see the screen over her shoulder. I skimmed it as I asked, "What kind of price did the owner put on it?"

"Let's see." She ran her finger across the field of data. "Here we are. Fifteen thousand an acre."

My jaw dropped open, but I don't know if it was because of the price or the fact I spotted the name of the property owner in the top left-hand corner of the screen, Stewart Edney!

She turned to me and frowned when she saw the surprise scribbled across my face. "Are you all right?"

"Huh? Oh, yeah, yeah, I'm fine," I hastily replied, trying to recover the role I was playing. "What did you say they were asking for the property?"

"Fifteen thousand an acre," she said sweetly. "And according to Mr. Charbonneau—he's the office manager— cheap at that price."

I whistled softly and gave her a smile. "Maybe so, but that's a little more than I had in mind. Thanks anyway."

Thirty minutes later I was back at the house, presenting Jack a flexible plastic rod with tiny fingers on one end, specifically designed for slithering under casts.

While he was contentedly scratching away, I deposited my gear, along with my .38, in an upstairs bedroom of the old mansion's second addition that was supposed to have been constructed in 1836. There were two doors to the bedroom, one opening to a narrow stairway that led below to a storage room adjoining the dining room. The second door opened onto the side gallery on the second floor, which led to the door opening to the circular stairs leading down to the lobby.

The bed was a four-poster with the requisite mosquito netting of the period, which fortunately was unnecessary because of the air conditioning unit fitted snugly in one window.

I placed my laptop on an ancient writing desk, one so old the scars were dark.

A grin played over my face when I spotted my e-mail from Eddie Dyson. The grin faded when I read his charge, three hundred dollars. I shook my head. "Doesn't look like much, Eddie. Not for three hundred bucks," I muttered as I read through it, then printed it on my portable ink jet.

I read back over the information as it emerged from the printer.

WR owed almost a quarter of a million on his business, half of which was in arrears. On top of that, he and his wife, Dorene, had divorced each other twice and remarried. Currently, they were divorced for the third time.

Stewart, gay as the sky is blue, owed the same bank over a hundred thousand, twenty of which was in arrears. In addition to regularly attending gay conventions in New Orleans, he sported a lengthy arrest record in the City of Sin, but strangely enough, none in Vicksburg. The former record must have been the *shame to the family* to which Annebelle had referred the day before; the latter, or lack thereof, a tribute to the power of money in a small city.

Of the three, money did not appear to be a motive for Annebelle. She owned her home, a small, neat brick in Old Town, and possessed a modest bank account. Still, there are some who are not content merely to possess a simple home and modest bank account.

Maybe she was one of those.

I leaned back and studied the report, disappointed in the

lack of substance. Still, it provided me another avenue to explore, the debt of the older brothers. As far as Annebelle was concerned, I could see no glaring financial motive for killing her father. Her brothers? Well, that was a different matter.

From the obvious acrimony displayed the day before between the three, there was no question in my mind that if Annebelle Edney spotted either of her brothers lying dead in the street, she would not hesitate to simply step over him and go on her merry way.

And neither was there a shred of doubt in my mind that they would gleefully reciprocate, leaving her behind without a thought.

Without warning, the patter of gently falling rain sounded on the wood shake roof. The rain grew heavier. Rain gusted across the gallery outside my door so I took the back stairs and cut through the dining room to the parlor.

As I passed the dining room table, I spotted the sympathy cards I'd opened for Jack the day before. I paused long enough to scoop them up. No reason I shouldn't talk to some of them. Perhaps they could provide me with some useful information.

I was skimming over them when a severe voice demanded, "May I help you?"

Glancing around, I saw a slight woman in a dark dress with a white lace collar. Her thin face wore a frown, and her gray hair was pulled back into a severe bun on the back of her head. She was *prim* personified. I nodded. "You must be Alice."

She pursed her lips.

"I'm Tony Boudreaux, a friend of Jack's. I'm the one who drove him over from Austin." I glanced at the ceiling. "He put me in the upstairs bedroom."

Her face softened. "I didn't know Mr. Jack had a guest."

"Sorry. We should have let you know." I don't know why I felt the urge to apologize, but it just seemed the thing to do.

With a brief nod, she said, "Would you care for some tea, Mr. Boudreaux? Fresh made. I'm getting some for Mr. Jack."

For a moment, I started to decline, but despite it being the middle of the summer, the drizzle running down the outside of the windows sent a chill through me. "Sure. Sounds good."

She nodded. "I'll bring it to you in the parlor with Mr. Jack's."

I stopped her. "Alice, can I talk to you a few moments first?"

She nodded, a puzzled look on her face. I guessed her to be in her seventies or so, but she had aged well. "Certainly, sir."

"You probably knew more about John Edney than anyone."

She cast a sidelong glance at the parlor. "I knew him very well. Probably better than his own children."

I picked up a nuance of resentment in her tone. Then I remembered the will. I tried not to push too fast. "How long had you been with him?"

Her response was instantaneous. "Eighteen years, six months, and fourteen days. Never sick once. I always had his meals on time, kept his house clean, and his clothes fresh. Not once did Mr. Edney ever complain."

"He must have been satisfied. He included you in his will."

Her eyes narrowed. "How did you know that? What business is it of yours?"

"Jack and I are old friends. I'm a private investigator back in Texas. Jack couldn't believe his father was so careless that he killed himself in an accident. He wanted to look into it."

Her glaring suspicion turned into a frown. "Look into it?" Her frown deepened as she absorbed the implication of my remarks. "You think it wasn't an accident?"

With a shrug, I replied, "I can't say. Any information pertinent to Mr. Edney's death, I have to turn over to the Vicksburg Police Department. They make the call."

She drew a deep breath, then slowly released it. "Yes, he included me in his will. I haven't seen it, but that's what he told me." Her brows knitted in anger and her words reeked with sarcasm. "He said I was in his will for the grand sum of ten thousand dollars." She shook her head, her words exploding in anger. "Can you imagine, Mr. Boudreaux? I took care of that man for eighteen years, six months, and fourteen days—better than his worthless children have ever done, and all he leaves me is ten thousand dollars." She shook her head. Tears welled in her eyes. "You know, I could have taken some of the silver or other valuables and sold them on eBay or at some flea market. Nobody would have known."

I felt her hurt, and her anger. "No. They probably wouldn't."

She gave me a rueful grin and wiped at the tears in her eyes. "Don't misunderstand. I'm not crying because of him, but because I'm mad at myself, and I don't know why. I guess it's because I feel like I've wasted eighteen years of my life. You know, I don't guess I should have, but I expected more." She drew a deep breath and slowly released it. "Mr. Edney, well, he was the only family I had. I just expected more from him." She drew another deep breath, then sighed in resignation. "Well, there's nothing I can do about it now, is there?"

"I suppose not, but you could answer a few more questions for me."

Pulling herself erect, she nodded. "Certainly. What do you want to know?"

"Tell you what, Alice. Bring me the tea in the parlor. Bring some for yourself too. We'll have us a little visit."

A look of alarm showed in her face. "But, Mr. Jack. He's in there."

I winked at her. "He was the one who started this whole thing."

She nodded. "If you say so. Just you go up in the parlor, and I'll be right back."

Chapter Eleven

Jack looked up from a rerun of "I Love Lucy" when I entered the parlor. His face wreathed in ecstasy, he was scratching under his cast with the slender rod. "Well, you get settled in?"

Nodding, I sat in a Victorian wingback upholstered in red velvet and trimmed with ornately carved rosewood. I laid the stack of sympathy cards on the end table. "As well as could be expected." I glanced around the parlor, noting the heavy tan drapes on the French doors and the intricately detailed wallpaper. "You were right about one thing. This is an old house."

At that moment, Alice entered with the tea. I'm no expert on tea services, but having escorted Janice Coffman-Morrison to several of her Aunt Beatrice's receptions, I had seen many expensive silver tea services, and the set Alice carried would suffer no shame in comparison.

She placed the tray on the coffee table, then carefully placed coasters before us on the Carrara marble for our tea as I spoke to Jack. "I asked Alice to sit with us. I want to bring you up to date on what's happening, and I want to hear her view of what's been going on around here the last few years."

Jack arched a quizzical eyebrow. "Fine with me."

I preferred no lemon nor milk nor sugar; the latter Jack ladled into his tea.

Alice sat on the edge of the Victorian couch across the coffee table from us, her tea perched on her knees. That she was uncomfortable was obvious.

I did not plan to reveal any details of why I believed the old man was murdered. While I was not suspicious of Jack, I knew how he blabbed when he had a little too much bourbon in his blood.

Consequently, all I did was bring him up to date on his father's wealth. "A possible twenty, maybe twenty-three million."

His eyes grew wide. "Twenty-three million? You got to be kidding. I was expecting six or eight, but twenty-three?"

"That's including the land south of Vicksburg," I explained. I turned to Alice. "What about that land? You ever hear any talk about the value of the riverside property south of here?"

She glanced at Jack and hesitated.

He smiled. "It's all right, Alice. If you heard anything, you can tell us."

She drew a deep breath. "From time to time," she whispered.

I had to lean forward to hear her.

"What did you hear?" Jack asked.

She looked from one of us to the other. "Well, Mr. Jack, about ten years ago, your father came in and announced that some idiot—those were his words—some idiot had insisted on buying that property." She paused.

Impatiently, Jack prompted her. "And?"

"And that was all he said. That day."

Jack frowned, confused.

Alice continued. "Then some days later, I heard him tell WR and Stewart about the offer. Now, you understand, I wasn't deliberately eavesdropping, but they were at the noon dinner table while I was clearing the dishes. I couldn't help hearing."

I nodded. "We understand. Go on."

"Mr. WR, he said something about the government thinking about building itself a highway, and Mr. Edney should sell the land. Mr. Edney wouldn't hear of it. The boys kept trying to talk him into selling the property, but he refused." She paused, glanced at Jack and me, then added, "They were getting awful loud when I left the dining room. I could hear them still arguing when I was way back in the kitchen although I couldn't make out what they were saying."

"Did you ever learn why he refused to sell the property?" I sat my unfinished tea on the coffee table, careful to use the coaster so the marble top would not stain.

She shook her head. "No, sir. I never did."

Jack spoke up. "Did my brothers keep after him to sell it?"

The older woman gave me a worried glance. I smiled and nodded. She continued. "From time to time, Mr. Jack, I'd hear the land mentioned. I couldn't swear on the Bible, but I felt like they were after him all the time to sell it. I supposed they knew how much it was worth."

Jack leaned forward. "What made you think that?"

She pondered her reply for several moments. "Hard to say. The way he always talked, he wasn't going to sell it— even when Stewart begged him."

"Begged him?"

"Yes, sir. Mr. Stewart, he had some bad gambling debts." She paused and looked from Jack to me. "Understand, I wasn't deliberately eavesdropping. I just . . ." She hesitated and glanced nervously from one to the other of us.

I nodded. "We know. Go on, Alice."

She directed her answer to Jack. "Well, Mr. Jack, about six months or so back, Mr. Stewart came in one afternoon and wanted to borrow some money. From what I heard, he owed a sizeable amount out at the Riverboat Casino. Mr. Edney refused. They had a terrible argument."

"Then what?"

"I was in the kitchen. I couldn't help hearing them. Honest. They were screaming at each other."

Jack nodded. "Go on."

"Well, Mr. Stewart kept shouting for his father to sell the land, and Mr. Edney said he had other plans for it. Then I heard Mr. Stewart say everyone would be better off if his father was dead. Mr. Edney screamed at Stewart to get out, to get out and not come back." She shook her head. "My heart just froze up at the terrible things they were saying to each other. It was so bad that Mr. Stewart didn't come back until just two or three weeks ago."

Clearing his throat, Jack inquired, "Did they argue again?"

Alice shook her head. "No. Mr. Edney just said he wasn't going to change his mind. What was done, was done."

"You didn't hear what he meant about not changing his mind?"

Her thin face wrinkled in concentration. "I can't put my finger on anything exactly, but I had the feeling he was planning on giving the land away."

Jack arched an eyebrow at me. "To his family. That stands to reason."

Alice shook her head slowly. "No, sir. Not to his children. To somebody else."

Surprised by her revelation, I leaned forward. "Who to?"

She shrugged. "I don't know, sir. I never heard Mr. Edney say it like that. It was just, well, just a feeling I got when I heard Mr. WR say he and Stewart could put the land to better use."

"Better use? Any idea what he meant by that?"

Alice shook her head. "I don't know."

I veered away from the riverside property. "Did Mr. Edney have many visitors?"

"You mean regular like?"

"Yes."

"He didn't entertain, if that's what you mean. He never asked me to serve tea or anything like that. Lordy no. Once, early on after he hired me, he had a visitor, and I asked if he wanted some refreshments. In no uncertain terms he told me no. That he don't want me to ever bother him when he had visitors." She drew a breath, then sighed deeply. "After that, whenever Mr. Edney had himself a visitor, I stayed out of sight unless he called me."

Later, after Alice returned to the kitchen to prepare an evening meal for Jack and me before she left for the day, he nodded in her direction. "What do you think about her story? You think she's trying to stir up trouble?"

Leaning against the velvet-covered back of the wing chair, I replied, "Why would she lie?"

Jack winced and poked the plastic rod under his cast at the wrist. He was becoming quite an artist in the way he could work that thin shaft deep into the confines of his cast. "This itches something terrible." Then he started poking around his shoulder. "You ever had to wear one of these things?"

I chuckled. "I never got drunk and fell off a stage. You better not break that off inside. They might really have to cut the cast off after all."

He glared at me. "You know where you can go." He returned to scratching at his wrist. "You want to know why I think she's trying to cause trouble? Ten thousand lousy bucks. She probably figured on at least a hundred thousand. Lord knows John could have afforded it." He shook his head. "He was a cheap miser."

I remained silent, considering the information Alice had passed along to us. I didn't know if the old man was cheap, but he was certainly private.

Jack broke into my thoughts. "So what do you think?"

Picking up the stack of sympathy cards from the end table, I idly thumbed through them while trying to assemble my thoughts in some sort of logical order. "I'm not sure. There are so many loose ends. And it seems as if they all contradict each other." I paused and gave him a sheepish grin. "If that makes sense."

Jack laughed. "Anything makes sense to me now, especially after learning how rich John was. Why, do you realize you are talking to a real millionaire, a multimillionaire?" He hesitated. A frown wrinkled his forehead, erasing the laughter on his face. "But you know something, Tony. I'm not happy over it. Not at all. I've got the weirdest feeling that there's something bad, something wrong about it all." He looked at me earnestly. "What about you?"

I paused rifling through the sympathy cards. The difference between Jack and me was that I didn't have that feeling because I knew something was wrong. I just didn't know what it was. "About all I know right now is that I've stumbled across a few questions that I'd like to find answers for."

His frown deepened. "Such as?"

With a wry chuckle, I began thumbing through the sympathy cards once again as I replied noncommittally, "I don't even know that exactly." I paused, staring at the card in my hand, the Madison Parish Ornithological Society, signed by Abigail Collins, Director. I looked up at Jack. "Have you gone through these cards?"

He ran his tongue under his bottom lip and dropped his eyes. "Not really. Just glanced at them. Why?"

I handed him the card from the ornithological society. "Your father had a lot of different friends. Take a look. This one's the birdwatchers. Take a look at this one. North End Rotary. Here's one from the First National Bank; the Vicksburg Unitarian Church; the Committee for Vicksburg Reconstruction; and Friends of the National Park Service."

Jack pursed his lips when he looked up at me. "So?"

"So. I don't think it will hurt to visit some of these people." I took the cards from him and dropped them in the pocket of my jacket and slipped the will and other documents in the other pocket. "Now," I said, rising, "first thing I need to do is get the window in my truck replaced. Then I'll start making my rounds."

"What about my brothers and sister? When are you going to talk to them?"

I considered his question. "I'll catch them one at a time, either at work or home."

* * *

While the glazier replaced my window, I called Diane, getting her answering machine. I suggested dinner at one of the casinos along the riverbank at eight, left my cell number, and as soon as my pickup was ready, headed across the river to Richmond, Louisiana, and the Madison Parish Ornithological Society.

Traffic on I-20 was heavy that afternoon, but flowed smoothly. I flexed my fingers about the steering wheel, wondering just what dealings John Wesley Edney had with the ornithological society.

Never having cultivated any interest in birdwatching, I had preconceived notions about the director, Abigail Collins. Probably a meek, dumpy matron with a sweet smile and a penchant for hot tea. An appropriate image for the name.

Was I ever surprised.

Chapter Twelve

Turning down a quaint street lined with ancient magnolias, I spotted the Madison Parish Ornithological Society's building off to the left.

It was a copy of Jefferson's Monticello, a Renaissance villa of red brick and white columns complete with the dramatic French dome.

I couldn't help admiring the classic architecture, at the same time bemused by its incongruous appearance in a neighborhood of dilapidated shotgun shacks.

I stopped in front of the receptionist, introduced myself, and asked to speak with Miss Abigail Collins. In a cool manner, and an almost indifferent tone, she asked the purpose of the visit.

"In regard to the death of John Wesley Edney," I explained.

Her cool manner vanished. A hint of pink tinged her cheeks. She rose quickly. "Yes, sir, Mr. Boudreaux. Just one moment, please."

Puzzled, I watched her hurry into an adjoining office. What had gotten her so excited? Surely she was aware of the old gentleman's death. They'd sent a sympathy card.

Moments later the door opened. Heels clicking sharply on

the terrazzo floor and her shoulder-length dark hair flowing behind her, a slender woman in her late thirties who would have had my vote as Miss America strode purposely toward me. I glanced past her for podgy Miss Abigail. The only one behind Miss America was the nervous secretary.

She stopped in front of me. Her dark eyes blazed fire. "Mr. Boudreaux?"

"Yes."

Her light green eyes narrowed, and her well-defined jaw hardened. "I'm Abigail Collins, and I can't say that I am pleased to meet you."

You could have knocked me over with Jack's broken emu feather. I had no idea what she was talking about. All I could do was gape.

Her eyes blazed.

Finally, I managed to overcome my surprise and shock. "You have me at a disadvantage, Miss Collins." I took a step backward. "Obviously, you're upset about something, but I haven't the slightest idea what."

"Oh, you don't, do you? Don't you represent John Wesley Edney?"

"Represent?" I shook my head. "No. I'm a private investigator looking into his death."

The anger fled from her face, replaced with a puzzled frown. "Investigator?"

I glanced over her shoulder at the curious young receptionist who was straining to hear our conversation. "Is there someplace we can talk? Privately."

She realized the receptionist was behind her. "Oh, yes. In my office. Please. This way." As she turned, she spoke to her receptionist. "Hold any calls, Marsha."

"Impressive place you have here," I said, following her into her office. "I've never visited Monticello." I gestured to the windows that were set near the floor. "Is this what the real place is like?"

A pleased smile dimpled her cheeks as she slipped into her chair behind the desk and nodded to another in front of her desk. "Isn't it beautiful? I wish I could say I was responsible for the idea, but the idea belonged to Wilson Jenkins, the previous director of the society. I took his place when he retired two years ago. He is such a wonderful man. I—" She caught herself. Her cheeks colored. "I mean, we really miss him around here." She glanced appreciatively around the room, her eyes settling on the windows. "Jefferson worked on Monticello for forty years. He set the windows close to the floor so that from outside, the house gives the appearance of a three-story building."

I frowned.

With a warm smile, she continued. "Take a look when you leave. In the other wings, windows are set higher, and those in the dome create the illusion of three stories."

The room in which we sat was impressive. I said as much.

With a soft laugh, she replied, "It wasn't cheap."

"Jenkins must have had some generous donors."

Her smile faded into a frown. "He did. One in particular. John Wesley Edney."

I attributed her frown to his death. I pulled out the sympathy card. "I saw the card you sent his children. They appreciated it very much." The last was a lie, but I figured anyone who sent a card should believe it was appreciated.

Her next remark almost knocked me out of my chair. "Had I known then what I learned yesterday, I would have saved the postage." The fire I'd seen earlier in her eyes blazed once again.

I forced a chuckle. "I'm sorry, Miss Collins. I don't understand."

Her eyes scrutinized me. Slowly, the anger faded from her eyes. "You really don't, do you?"

"I wish I did. What happened to upset you?"

"Upset?" She drew a deep breath. "How about infuriated, enraged, outraged?"

I gave her a crooked grin. "Okay. I'll go along with infuriated. I don't know about outraged, but infuriated works for me," I replied flippantly.

She glared at me a moment, then a tiny smile ticked up the edge of her lips. She gave her head a brief shake. "Please excuse me, Mr. Boudreaux, but—"

"Call me Tony. Like they always say, Mr. Boudreaux is my father. I'm just Tony."

Her smile grew wider. "All right, Tony. I'm Abigail, Abby to my friends."

"Nice to know you, Abby. Now, fill me in on what's going on. What happened yesterday?"

She paused a moment. "I told you that Mr. Edney donated the funds for this building. You see, he and Wilson—" She hesitated, and a slight blush covered her cheeks. "I mean he and Mr. Jenkins had known each other for years. Mr. Edney was one of our most generous benefactors. Then yesterday, I learned that the offer of land he had promised the society for a preserve had been withdrawn."

"Promised?"

She nodded.

"Verbal or in writing?"

"In writing."

"What's the problem then? If it's in writing, take it to court."

She arched an eyebrow. "Yes, but that's another problem. It was in his will. He gave us a copy of his will several years ago just after he promised us the land."

I frowned. "He what? Did you say he gave you a copy of his will?"

"Yes."

"Why would he do that?"

She shrugged. "I had just started working here, and I asked Mr. Jenkins that very question. He said Mr. Edney wanted the society to know he was serious about his promise." A crooked smile played over her lips. "It didn't really make much sense to me, but I didn't worry about it. Then yesterday, I learned he had changed the will. All the land is going to his children."

The hair on the back of my neck bristled. Land. Children.

"Are you talking about the riverside land south of Vicksburg?"

She looked at me in surprise. "Why yes. How did you know?"

"I read the will also."

She grimaced. "It was to be a bird sanctuary. It's the home of three birds on the endangered lists, the *Limnothlypis swainsonii*—" She hesitated when she spotted the confused look on my face. "Sorry," she said with a sheepish grin. "I should have said a Swainson's Warbler, Kentucky Warbler, and Prothonotary Warbler. The Prothonotary is also known as Golden Swamp Warbler." She shook her head. "It is one of the most beautiful birds I have ever seen. And," she added, "the land is also a stopover in the northern and southern flyways for a sanctuary like that. I was stunned when I read the new will."

"That was one of the big surprises in the will," I replied. "The boys, WR and Stewart, wanted Mr. Edney to sell the property. He refused. No one knew exactly why, but his housekeeper told us that she had the feeling he was going to give it to someone."

Abby frowned. "That would be us. But, why did he change his mind?"

All I could do was shrug. I pulled out my copy of the new will. "Here's the new one. According to it, your organization is included for a sum of ten thousand dollars."

"Ten thou—" She clamped her lips shut. Tears brimmed in her eyes. Fighting the emotion threatening to sweep over her, she sighed. "I suppose I should be happy for that, but the preserve would have been a tremendous environmental asset to the area, helping to preserve part of the ecology as well as American wildlife."

"And you say he gave the society a copy of the will?"

"Yes. Would you care to see it?"

"If you don't mind." To me, it was a little more than odd. The old man must have not only been eccentric, but eccentric with a capital E. On the other hand, anyone worth $23 million could, like the six-hundred-pound gorilla, do just about whatever he wanted to do.

Retrieving it from a desk drawer, she handed the document to me. "The date on it is in his hand."

At an upward slant across the top left corner of the will was the date, July 11, 1993. Eleven years ago. I skimmed the will. It was identical to the new one with two exceptions. Madison Parish Ornithological Society was beneficiary of the thousand and ten acres, and Annebelle Edney's name was not mentioned.

I glanced at the new will and date on which it had been signed, July 24, 2004.

"July twenty-fourth," I muttered. "And the fire was on the twenty-sixth." I pursed my lips and studied the will, hoping for some revelation, which never came. "Two days later."

"My secretary said you were here in regard to his death. Exactly what did you mean by that?"

"One of his sons, the younger one, asked me to look into the events surrounding his father's death. That's all I'm doing. I found your sympathy card and saw your organization in his will, so I naturally wondered what he was doing with a group of, of ah—" I hesitated, not knowing exactly what to call them without offending her.

She chuckled. "Birdwatchers?"

I shrugged. "Yeah."

She studied me a moment. "Why would his son want the death investigated? I heard it was an accident." She leaned forward, an inquisitive frown on her slender face. A flash of excitement flared in her eyes. "He doesn't believe it was an accident?"

I tried to sidestep her question. "He doesn't know. He just wants to be sure."

A tiny grin curled her lips as her twinkling eyes tried to search deep into my own. She went for the jugular. "Let me ask you. If it weren't an accident, but deliberate—would that change the will?"

I shrugged. "Beats me. But I don't see how." I changed the subject. "Apparently, Mr. Edney had given no indication he was considering changing his will."

"That's right."

"When was the last time you saw him?"

She pondered my question. "At the last board meeting in February."

"He didn't mention a new will?"

"No."

"He have any close friends in the society?"

She shook her head. "Not after Mr. Jenkins retired."

"How can I get in touch with Mr. Jenkins?"

She quickly sketched a map and jotted some numbers. "His place is on the Louisiana side of the river across from the land we were promised. Here are the directions and his phone number." She paused. A slight blush tinged her cheeks once again. "He's such a sweet man. Tell him I said 'hi' and not to be a stranger."

I pointed my finger at her like a pistol. "You got it."

Outside, I paused to study the façade of the Monticello lookalike before climbing in the Silverado. Abby was right. The building did appear to be three stories.

I was never much of an historian, but in Louisiana where I was reared, those of us with Acadian ancestries always had a warm spot for Thomas Jefferson. After all, had it not been for him, we might still belong to France. "Perish the thought," I muttered as I climbed into the pick-up. I paused before starting the engine, chuckling over the disclaimer French's Foods had issued when the anti-France sentiment swept across the country. *The only thing our mustard has in common with France is they are both yellow.*

Thank you again, Thomas Jefferson.

Back on the interstate, I was too absorbed with my own thoughts to see the eighteen-wheelers boxing me in.

Chapter Thirteen

When I'm working a case, I talk to myself as I drive. I don't mean I simply mull the situation. I actually talk, aloud, asking questions and then answering them. Somehow the spoken word creates a more solid impression in my pea-sized brain than a simple thought.

More than once as I've been driving, I've had the uncom-fortable feeling someone was staring at me, only to look around square into the laughing eyes of those in a passing vehicle.

And that's exactly what I was doing during the drive to Wilson Jenkins' home. I was deep into conversation with myself about the motivations of my suspects—WR, Stewart, and Annebelle—when I noted the eighteen-wheeler pulling a car carrier ahead of me was slowing.

I glanced in my side mirror in anticipation of pulling around the rig, but staring me right in the eye was the blunt nose of a howling Peterbilt coming up on my left. I pulled back to await his passing.

Except that when he drew even with me, he slowed.

I was uncomfortable to be in such close proximity to the two large rigs, so I started to back away until I spotted the snarling grill of a Kenworth coming up behind.

Muttering a soft curse, I maintained my speed. Then, to

my alarm, I noticed the rig behind wasn't slowing. He was moving up on me until the shiny grill filled my mirror.

"All right, boys," I mumbled, growing antsy. "Have your fun, then let's move on." My hands began to sweat. I flexed my fingers about the steering wheel. I noted the Texas license plate on the car carrier in front of me. They might be just having fun with local yokels on the road, but this was one local yokel who planned to report them. I committed the license to memory.

The rig behind crept closer.

Then, as one, the rigs in front and beside me increased their speed. I remained at sixty until the Kenworth on my tail tapped my bumper. My head snapped back then popped forward. I struggled to straighten the swerving pickup.

I had no choice but to speed up with them.

In less than a minute, we were hitting ninety.

Finally, after a couple of miles, the rig behind me began backing away. I breathed a sigh of relief until from the corner of my eye, I saw the Peterbilt on my left edging into my lane, forcing me off the road.

At ninety miles an hour.

"Better think fast, Tony," I mumbled, keeping one eye on the rig in front, one on the eighteen-wheeler at my side, and the third on the one behind.

Suddenly, I realized what they had in mind. Except this time, I wasn't dodging a bag of cement. I had to move fast before they could carry out their plan. That was my only chance to beat them at their own game—if I wasn't already too late. I had no idea what lay ahead, but I had no choice.

Abruptly, I jerked my pickup onto the shoulder and slammed on the brakes. The rigs shot past, but I didn't have time to pay them attention. Directly ahead, an old pickup was parked on the shoulder, the one someone had put there just for me. To my right was a shallow drop off, just deep enough to send me tumbling end over end.

Clenching my teeth, I did my best to stomp the brake pedal through the floor. The sixteen-inch tires screamed in agony as the graveled shoulder peeled away layers of rubber in a cloud of smoke.

The rear of the pickup loomed ever larger.

"Hang on, Tony," I muttered through clenched teeth. "Hang on." I squeezed the wheel so tightly my knuckles turned white. I quickly calculated, then hastily rejected trying to squeeze between the pickup and ditch. No way I could make it.

The needle on the speedometer swung down to seventy, dropped to fifty, then thirty.

By now, the pickup was no more than forty feet in front of me. There was no way I could stop in time. In desperation, I cut the wheels sharply to the left, sending the Silverado into a broadside slide.

I closed my eyes and braced for the impact.

Mercifully, it never came.

When I opened my eyes, I was still alive. Shaking, I climbed from the Silverado and walked unsteadily around to see how much room I had to spare. I whistled softly. "That was close," I muttered, staring at the three-inch space between the rusty bumper and the door on the passenger's side.

At that moment, a Louisiana Highway Patrol cruiser pulled up. A tall, beefy man stepped out and nodded to the Silverado. "Trouble?" He eyed me suspiciously.

"Not now, Officer." I didn't have time for delays, so I shaded the truth. I pointed to the rigs now disappearing around a curve. "One of those rigs up there accidentally ran me off the road. I don't think he even knew he did it," I explained. "I was lucky I stopped when I did."

He continued to eye me suspiciously. "May I see your license and insurance, sir?"

He studied them, then looked back at me. "You been drinking?"

"No, sir." I hooked my thumb over my shoulder, grateful I had left my .38 back in my room. "You can look through the pickup if you want."

He wanted.

He searched the pickup thoroughly, then he opened the tool chest in the bed. He pulled out a black satchel. "What's in here?"

"Tools of the trade," I explained. "I'm a private investigator in Austin, Texas. There's a tape recorder, camcorder, various bugging devices, flashlight, bugs, sweepers, odds and ends."

He rummaged through the satchel, then returned it to the tool chest. His eyes grew wide. "Well, well, well," he muttered, holding up a half-empty pint of Jim Beam bourbon.

My eyes almost popped out. I shook my head adamantly. "Look, Officer, that isn't mine. I don't know how it got there."

He nodded, a disgusted look on his face. "That's what they all say. Would you step over to my cruiser, please?"

By now, I was getting worried. Louisiana jails were notorious. Louisiana police even more so.

Rumor had it that confiscating vehicles was such a popular hobby among many of the law officers that some had even considered mounting them on their walls. Of course, I didn't believe that, but I sure didn't want to take a chance. "Why?"

"You have any objection to a sobriety test, Mr. Boudreaux?" He slipped my driver's license and insurance form in his shirt pocket.

"Of course not," I replied in what I hoped was a firm, confident tone.

"But you do drink?"

"No longer. I'm in AA. I've been sober for three years." I conveniently left out the time I'd had a few sociable drinks at the family reunion on Whiskey Island in the Atchafalaya Swamp. Family reunions didn't count.

I accompanied him to his cruiser where he pulled out the Intoxilyzer for the breath test. I did as he instructed. His eyebrows rose as he read the results. "Well, Mr. Boudreaux, you were right." He returned my license and insurance. "That was a close call."

"I promise you one thing, Officer. If I'd been drinking, I would never have been able to stop."

For the first time, he smiled. "You get the license number on the rig that ran you off the road?"

I hesitated, then decided to keep the information to myself. "Sorry. I had other things on my mind. Staying alive mainly."

Chapter Fourteen

Ten minutes later, I found the road leading to Wilson Jenkins' place. He lived in a neat cottage on a slope overlooking the Mississippi River. I had been one hundred and eighty degrees off in the image I had conjured up in my head about Abigail Collins, so I was somewhat surprised when Wilson Jenkins turned out to be exactly what I imagined a male birdwatcher to be: Slender, thinning hair, soft-spoken, an amiable grin on his face. Like a tiny sparrow.

He invited me into a sunroom facing the river where he poured us each a glass of lemonade. We sat on a comfortable leather couch facing a broad span of windows overlooking the river. Pictures of every imaginable bird covered the walls, from tiny bluebirds to diving hawks with outstretched claws ready to rip and tear.

I explained the purpose of my visit. "You and Mr. Edney had known each other for years according to Miss Collins, who by the way asked me to tell you 'hi and not to be such a stranger.' "

A slight blush colored his cheeks. He ducked his head. "She's a fine woman." He cleared his throat. "Now, how can I help you?"

"You knew him for a long time, right?"

81

"All our lives. We grew up together. We often talked about a preserve for the endangered birds."

"I suppose you heard about the new will?"

His gentle smile faded. "I couldn't believe it when Abby told me. She called me last night. Poor thing was in tears. JW had never in his life gone back on his word." He shook his head. "I was stunned, Mr. Boudreaux. Stunned."

"I've seen the new will. It differs in two places from the old one. In the new one, the land was bequeathed to his children, and Annebelle Edney is included. Did he ever mention either of those changes to you?"

"Never. Last time anything was said about the will was when he gave it to us ten or eleven years ago. JW was funny like that. Eccentric you might say."

I arched an eyebrow. *Eccentric!* An understatement if I'd ever heard one. "Why would he give the society a copy of his will? Abby said it was because he wanted the society to know that he was serious about what he had promised."

Jenkins hesitated, his thin face screwed in concentration. He rose and walked to the window and stared out over the river. "I never could figure out why he was so obsessed with proving to people he meant what he said he was going to do." He turned back to me. "Does that make sense?"

His meaning evaded me. "Not really."

He scratched his head. "It was something more with JW. He could have simply told us he was bequeathing the land to the society, but he took it a step forward and gave us a copy of the will. Like I said, eccentric. You see what I'm trying to say?"

"Sorry. I suppose I'm just dense."

He returned to his seat on the couch. "Ask anyone who knew JW. If he told someone he was going to—" He paused, then shook a thin finger at me. "I remember several years ago. He wanted to buy an old Model T from a farmer near Jackson—a little Runabout if my memory serves me correctly. I was with him when he told the man over the phone he would be out the next week to buy it. As soon as he hung up, he sat down and wrote the same man a letter stating exactly what he had said on the telephone." He paused. "Would you do something like that?"

I shook my head, remembering the sheath of letters in JW's personal files, letters that confirmed commitments he had made to various individuals.

"Nor would I," Jenkins replied. "You see what I mean by eccentric?"

For a few moments, I pondered his question. Slowly, I began to see the point he was trying to make. "What you're trying to say is—"

"I'm not trying to say anything except that for him to make such a change in the will and then not follow up on it with a letter or note of confirmation to those affected was not at all like JW. Not one bit."

It was my turn to rise and cross the room to the window. The muddy waters of the Mississippi churned slowly past. Even from our location on the crest of a hill half a mile distant from the river, I could make out the giant swirls generated by the violent currents below the surface.

I felt as if I was caught up in its vortex, helpless in my struggle against the rips and whirlpools of intrigue while I tried to nail down solid evidence.

Still, I had more to go on now than I did only a few hours earlier.

"More lemonade? Perhaps some cookies, oatmeal cookies? I'm not much of a baker, so I use ready-mix, but they are tasty. I usually bake sugar cookies, but oatmeal goes better with lemonade."

Turning back to him, I declined. "You baked them yourself, huh?"

"That's one of the penalties of being a bachelor, Mr. Boudreaux."

I looked around the neat cottage. On impulse, I reached for a cookie. "I think I will try one." Despite ready-mix, they were, as Jenkins said, tasty. "How come you never married?" I asked around a bite of oatmeal cookie.

"Never found the right woman," he said, his voice so soft I had to strain to hear him.

"Well," I replied with a good-natured grin, "what about Abigail Collins?"

He blushed. "Oh, dear me no. She is much too young, and too pretty."

"She thinks highly of you."

He gave me a surprised look. "I didn't know that."

Suddenly, I felt a tinge of sorrow for the shy, quiet little man who had probably lived his entire life in the shadows of the Neanderthal Beach Bully, missing out on life because of a reluctance to risk embarrassment by the rejection of a woman.

I remembered the blush that had come to Abby's cheeks at the mention of his name. "Trust me. Go see her."

When I left, I had a bounce in my step. It's a good feeling to think that perhaps you've made someone's life a little better.

On the other hand, I reminded myself growing sober, a second attempt had been made on my life.

Chapter Fifteen

Before driving away, I faithfully jotted my notes on three-by-five cards, pausing to reassess what I believed to be the salient points of my visit with Wilson Jenkins.

First, the preserve had been the subject of many discussions over the years by Jenkins and Edney. Second, JW Edney had made no mention of the two changes in the new will. And third, Edney was obsessive about following up promises with a letter of confirmation.

Why the latter?

I had no idea. And aberrant behavior always made me wary of any theories or conclusions I might draw.

But now, the only logical conclusion I could construe from the interview with Jenkins was that the changing of the will with no follow-up was indeed out-of-character behavior on the part of JW Edney.

Quickly, I glanced back over the growing stack of note cards. For some reason, I had the feeling I had overlooked some detail, but what?

As I shifted into gear and headed to the interstate, I pondered the old man's obsession with follow-up letters. What kind of person would do something like that? Obviously an individual to whom organization and details were important.

"Stop and think a moment, Tony," I said aloud. "If someone has the patience bordering on almost a maniacal obsession to take apart a Model T bolt-by-bolt and restore it to showroom quality, chances are they could be obsessive enough to write follow-up letters."

Then a revelation hit me. Those little flashes of insight don't happen too often for me, but when they do, I always pursue them. So, first chance I had, I would pay a visit to JW's attorney.

Back in Vicksburg, I stopped by Jack long enough to learn the location of WR's hardware store, which turned out to be on Washington Street also, a few doors beyond the original building housing the Biedenharn Candy Company where Coca-Cola was first bottled in 1894.

The building was in need of repair. Mortar crumbled from between the dingy red bricks, and the plate-glass show windows appeared to have had no acquaintance at all with soap and water.

In my brief encounter with WR the previous day, I realized he probably wasn't the brightest bulb on the string. The unimaginative name of his store, Washington Street Hardware, reinforced that opinion.

He scowled when he saw me enter. I looked about the store. It was empty of customers. A single clerk was leaning idly beside the manual cash register on the front counter. I couldn't believe this was what he owed the bank a quarter of a million on.

And I don't know how WR used the few hundred thousand his father had given him over the years, but it certainly wasn't to modernize the hardware store. The worn wooden flooring was split, uneven, and even springy in spots. Decades of dust darkened the ceiling.

I headed directly toward him.

"What do you want?" His tone was gruff and threatening.

"Just to visit a moment. That's all."

He started to walk away, but I stopped him with a white lie. "The police chief sent me."

WR froze, then looked around, a look of disbelief on his round face. "Police chief? You mean Hemings?"

I nodded. "I'll be blunt, WR. Someone murdered your father."

The look of disbelief grew more pronounced. "Murdered?" He snorted. "You're crazy."

"That isn't what Chief Hemings thinks. That's why he gave me his okay to follow through on the case."

WR studied me suspiciously, his shoulders thrown back and his belly straining against the light green shirt he wore. "Why you?"

I was candid with him. "Your brother didn't believe the fire was an accident. He hired me to find out."

"Jack? What made him think the fire wasn't an accident?"

"The way I understand it, he believed his father was too cautious, too careful for that kind of accident to occur."

He pondered my response a moment. "Okay. So why are you here—at my place?"

"Because you owe a quarter of a million to the bank, and you stand to inherit several million after the will is probated. That's motive enough in anyone's book." I waited for his reaction to my remark, several million. He didn't react, which told me he knew the value of the riverside land.

WR sputtered and tapped his middle finger against his chest. "You mean—you mean, you think I did it? That I killed my own father? That's a crock."

I watched for the family sign of nervousness, the tongue under the bottom lip, but it never appeared. "I didn't say you did. All I said was I wanted to talk to you about it. After all, you claimed you had no idea your father was going to leave you the riverside property."

He nodded emphatically. "That's right. That was a surprise to me, and to Stewart." He was growing belligerent, the way guilty people do. "He had planned to give it to some bird-watching group."

"What about the afternoon he died? The twenty-sixth? Where were you?"

He glared at me. "What business is it of yours?"

I shrugged. With a note of indifference in my voice, I replied, "Hey, tell me or tell Chief Hemings. I don't care."

His belligerence dried up, replaced by a worried look in his eyes. "All right, all right. I was over at Shreveport the day JW died. Me and Stewart."

"I suppose you have witnesses."

Now his tongue started moving along the inside of his bottom lip. "I told you, I was with Stewart."

"Come on, WR. Get real. How credible is your own brother when each of you stand to inherit five or six million? You think a jury will fall for that?"

The worry on his face deepened. His tongue didn't miss a beat.

"Who did you visit over there?"

He licked his lips. "That's the problem. Nobody. We went to a bar called the Tiger's Den."

I waited for him to continue. When he didn't I prompted him. "Okay. The Tiger's Den. Why did you go to the Tiger's Den? Is it a special kind of bar or something?"

A flash of anger turned his cheeks red. He glared at me. "What are you driving at? I don't go to *them* kind of bars."

"I don't know about Chief Hemings, but if I was the chief of police, I'd figure that's a long drive just to go to a bar."

WR hesitated. Sweat glistened on his flabby cheeks.

I was growing exasperated. "Look, you tell me, or you tell Hemings. I'm tired of fooling with you." I turned to walk away.

"Wait."

I halted.

He paused, then continued. "All right. Here's the truth." I turned back to him.

"The honest truth," he said, staring at the floor as he shifted his feet nervously. "We went to meet a lawyer who had called Stewart. The guy said he had pictures of JW with some bimbo in a hotel. For a cut of the inheritance, he said he would—" He hesitated. To give him some credit, his cheeks reddened with embarrassment. "If we agreed to give him twenty percent of our inheritance, he said he would go to JW and threaten to send the pictures to the newspapers and TV stations if JW did not deed the land over to us now."

"So you went to meet him?" I couldn't keep the disgust from my voice.

He continued staring at the floor. "Yeah."

I knew the answer to my next question, but I asked it anyway. "Why would your father care one way or another?"

Eyes blazing, WR looked up and snorted. "He was a religious nut. Town father. That sort of thing. He would have probably had a stroke if those pictures were published."

"Convenient for you and your brother, huh?"

The color in WR's cheeks deepened.

Things, to paraphrase *Alice in Wonderland*, were growing curiouser and curiouser. "Who is this guy?"

WR dropped his gaze back to the floor. "That's the problem," he said lamely, "he didn't show up."

"But, he gave you a name."

He shook his head. "No," he replied lamely.

"That's mighty convenient. Mighty convenient."

His eyes pleaded with me. "That's the gospel truth. Honest."

"All right. For the time being, it's the truth." His lip didn't move but I still didn't believe him for one second, not completely. But now that I had him in a talkative mood, I didn't want him to clam up. "What time were you to meet this lawyer?"

"Four o'clock. He didn't show. We got there about three, had a couple beers. When he wasn't there by six, we left."

I arched an eyebrow just so he would know I had serious doubts about his story. "What about Annebelle? Why didn't your father have her in the old will?"

Absently, he smoothed at his slick hair. "When we was kids, JW took a strap to us on a regular basis. Annebelle, as you probably noticed, can be outspoken and stubborn. Well, she never let the old man push her around." He chuckled. "Anyway, she got fed up and went to live with an aunt. Her and the old man didn't talk for years."

At that moment, the telephone rang. The young clerk answered, then held the receiver over his head. "For you, WR."

I watched as WR spoke into the receiver. He glanced in my direction, then turned his back to me. A cold chill ran down my spine. I was the topic of someone's clandestine conversation.

Upon his return, I gave no indication I knew I had been the subject of the call. Instead, I summarized his where-abouts on the night of July 26. "So, your story is that you and your brother drove to Shreveport to meet a lawyer who never showed, a lawyer whose name you don't even know?" He chewed on his bottom lip, then nodded, and I added with a trace of disgust in my tone. "One who would blackmail your father for you?"

He dragged the tip of his tongue over his dry lips. "Yes," he croaked.

"For a cut of your inheritance?"

"Yes."

Chapter Sixteen

I studied the rundown hardware store from the front seat of my pickup, pondering WR's account of his whereabouts the day of his father's death. He had motive, as did Stewart, and as far as I was concerned, if the Tiger's Den was his only alibi, then he also had opportunity.

Despite WR's remark the previous night that the land south of Vicksburg was worthless swamp, I figured they both knew the true value of the acreage. Otherwise, why would Stewart have placed it on the market? On the other hand, why put it on the market when it was not theirs to sell?

I chuckled when I thought of WR. He was probably burning up the telephone lines to Stewart and Annebelle.

As I drove away from the hardware store, my cell phone rang. It was Diane. "Just walked in from work. Got your message. I'd love to go out for old times' sake," she added with a giggle.

"Where?"

"How about the dining room at the Golden Fleece Casino Riverboat at the bottom of Clay Street. Eight o'clock all right?"

"Sounds good to me."

"I'll get us a table."

"Sounds even better. See you then." I clicked off, trying

unsuccessfully to ignore the guilt sweeping over me when I thought of Janice. After all, I told myself in an effort to rationalize my actions, we're not engaged or committed or anything. This isn't like I'm running around on her.

Of course, I didn't know what else I could call it, but I wasn't about to call it "running around on her."

I glanced at my watch: 4:45. Over three hours to kill. If I hurried, I could catch William Goggins, John Wesley Edney's attorney, to see if that flash of insight that hit me after I left Wilson Jenkins was indeed inspired or simply wishful thinking.

I headed south on Washington. As I passed Vicksburg Auto Parts, I made a note to come back after I took care of my business with Goggins.

William Goggins was the epitome of the courtroom lawyer, impeccably well groomed from manicured nails to freshly trimmed hair. His tanned face emanated confidence. Stylishly dressed in an Armani suit that had to set him back at least a couple of thousand, he was precise and articulate, possessing the genteel manners my mother had gallantly attempted, but miserably failed to instill in me.

His office had all the trappings of success. In a smooth, basso profundo voice, he graciously gestured to a red leather chair and said, "Please. Have a seat, Mr. Boudreaux. How can I assist you?"

After explaining my reason for being there and mentioning that I did have the blessing of Police Chief Field Hemings, I said, "Just a couple questions, Mr. Goggins. From what I've heard, the new will came as a big surprise to Stewart and WR Edney."

I don't know if a smile can be gentle or not, but that's what his was, gentle. I couldn't help wondering just how long it took him to perfect it. "Yes," he replied. "It even shocked me when JW called and asked me to write a new one with those new provisions."

"I see. When did he do that? Do you happen to remember?"

His tanned forehead wrinkled in concentration. "It was

either on the sixteenth or seventeenth of July, about a week before he came in to sign it on the twenty-fourth. Yes. I'd say the seventeenth."

I measured my next question carefully. "And after that call, did he communicate with you at all before he signed the will?"

Goggins frowned at the question. "I don't understand."

"I mean, did he communicate with you between the time he requested the new will and when he signed it?"

He shook his head, a puzzled frown on his tanned face. "Why, no. There was no need."

Aha! Sherlock Boudreaux now had a firm lead. No follow-up letter. Not much, but something. I continued my sly probing. "How long has Mr. Edney been your client, Mr. Goggins?"

"Around three years. He had been a long-term client of my deceased partner, Harvey Brittain. After Harvey's death, I parceled out some of our clients, but Mr. Edney was much too valuable to turn over to another attorney."

I chuckled. "I can understand that." I rose and extended my hand. "I appreciate your time." I hesitated, wondering just how well Lawyer Goggins knew his client. "One more question."

He nodded, and I continued. "After you took him on as your client three years ago, did he make any changes to the will prior to this last one or make any large purchases requiring the expertise of an attorney?"

"Nothing. Nothing at all."

Nodding slowly, I rose to my feet. "I guess that's all I need, Mr. Goggins. Thanks again." I turned to leave. He had given me much to consider. In fact, I was beginning to question his possible complicity in the murder. His portrayal of JW Edney in no way corroborated that of Wilson Jenkins. Someone was lying, and I had the overpowering hunch that it was William Goggins.

Five minutes later, I pulled in at the curb in front of the parts house. Doc Raines and JW Edney had been old friends. Maybe he could answer the question that had been nagging at me ever since I left Wilson Jenkins.

With an amiable grin on his round face, Doc Raines waved when he spotted me. "Well," he began, "you going to buy that little Runabout?"

"Haven't even asked yet, but if it's reasonable, I might just load it up on a trailer and haul it back to Austin."

He grew solemn. "How are JW's kids taking their father's death?"

"About the way you'd expect." I didn't suppose I was really lying. After all, he knew how stormy their relationships had been. "Got a question for you, Doc. About JW."

He raised an eyebrow. "Shoot."

"I was told he had the peculiar habit of writing a letter to confirm a previous decision." I paused.

Doc frowned. "I don't follow."

"It's like this. That Runabout. Another friend of his said that once he heard JW not only tell the owner he wanted to buy the car, but then the next day, he watched as JW also wrote the man a letter reaffirming his intentions."

His eyes lit in understanding. "Oh, that. Yeah. I've seen him do that. Not on small things, but larger ones, important decisions. Like the Runabout."

With a rueful chuckle, I said, "That seem kind of eccentric to you?"

Doc laughed. "Eccentric? How about nuts? I used to tease JW about that. Sure burned him up." He grimaced. "Sorry. I didn't mean it like that. I meant, when I teased him about those follow-up letters, it sure got under his skin." He grew solemn and slowly shook his head. He swallowed hard. "I wish that odd old man was here so I could tease him again."

"What made him do that? Any idea?"

He nodded. "Years ago, when we were both young and wild, JW met a pretty young thing who stole his heart. He was head over heels in love with her, but her old man wouldn't consider JW because he was footloose and poor. So, JW got himself a job driving a milk delivery truck for the dairy north of town. All the while, the old man allowed the young woman other suitors.

"Well, JW worked hard. He was determined to prove to the girl's father that he could take care of her. He found a piece of land with a small house. He told the owner he'd bring him a down payment, but when he got there a couple days later, the owner had already sold the house and land. He claimed since JW hadn't shown up, he had the right to change his mind. The girl married someone else. JW was crushed. Went on a two-week drunk, and afterward swore that whoever he was dealing with in the future would never be able to question his sincerity and determination."

I absorbed Doc's explanation. I didn't know if I agreed with JW's philosophy or not, but at least it gave some credence to why he was eccentric in such a manner.

Back in my pickup, I studied the restored building that housed the parts store. I was beginning to believe that this case had more loose ends than a Louisiana centipede has legs.

Chapter Seventeen

After my father, John Roney Boudreaux, deserted Mom and me, we moved in with Pa's folks, Moise and Ola Boudreaux. Often, *Grandpere* Moise took me hunting down in the swamps and forests where a soul always had to keep a careful eye out for alligators, wild boars, and cottonmouth water moccasins.

Those critters were nothing compared to the buzz saw I ran into when I went back to Jack's after leaving Goggins.

I was right. WR had called Stewart and Annebelle as soon as I left the hardware store. When I walked into the parlor, the three of them were yelling and screaming at Jack, whom they had backed against the wall between the two sets of French doors. He was fending them off with the plastic scratcher.

Jack spotted me. "Tony! Am I glad to see you."

As one, the three fell silent and turned to glare at me.

"There he is," WR muttered.

Annebelle took a step toward me. "What's all this non-sense about John being murdered?" Her tone was a mixture of defiance and belligerence.

I looked at WR. "I figured you would tell them."

"Any reason not to?"

"Just makes it easier for me," I said, keeping my voice soft. "Now I can talk to everyone at the same time."

Stewart was wearing a powder-blue hairdresser's blouse. He must have dropped his scissors and come running when WR called. The overhead light reflected off the sheen of sweat on his bald head. He sneered. "You're crazy if you think someone murdered John. He just got careless."

"What kind of proof you got?" Annebelle demanded.

I smiled amiably. "None."

Stewart frowned. "Then why are you investigating it at all?"

"Like I told WR, your brother hired me."

Jack pointed the arm scratcher at them. "John was not the kind to get careless. Now, I might be wrong. Maybe it was an accident." He paused. "I hope it was an accident, but wouldn't you want to know if someone did deliberately kill him?"

WR and Stewart looked at each other. "I suppose so," Stewart finally muttered. "But it wasn't one of us, and I don't have any idea who would have wanted to kill him."

Annebelle said nothing.

In a thin voice, WR said, "The way you talked at the store, it sounded like you thought maybe me or Stewart did it."

"No," I replied shaking my head. "I said you both, in fact, all four of you have reason enough to kill him, twenty-three million of them, but I didn't say you did."

Annebelle frowned. "What do you mean, twenty-three million?"

Jack spoke up. "John's estate. That land south of Vicksburg is a lot more valuable than we thought."

WR looked at Stewart in feigned surprise. He dragged his tongue under his bottom lip. "Did you hear that?"

Stewart tried to fake his own surprise. "I don't believe it." He glanced surreptitiously at me, then hastily looked away.

The expression on their faces told me the truth. They knew. They had known for years.

Annebelle snorted. "Well, we might have had words with John, but none of us would have killed him."

I ignored her protest. "I know where WR and Stewart were on the twenty-sixth. You mind telling me where were you?"

Her face grew red. "You accusing me?"

"Nope." I gave her what I hoped was a disarming grin. "Just asking questions. Either I ask them or the sheriff asks them."

She studied me a moment. "I was at Jackson, at a softball tournament. You can ask Nancy Carleton. She's the coach. I sat on the bench with her and hit balls to the infielders during warmups and then scouted teams we might play."

Stewart snorted. "Since when did you have anything to do with softball?"

Fire blazed from her eyes. "You don't know nothing about me, brother dear. At least I have an alibi."

I interrupted their sibling spat. "This Nancy Carleton. Does she live here in Vicksburg?"

Annebelle nodded, her frizzed hair bobbing up and down. "On Baldwin Ferry Road, forty-seven thirty-one." She gave me the telephone number. "Check with her. She'll tell you."

I glanced at Stewart who wore a smirk on his thick lips.

Annebelle continued. "We left Friday morning. That was the twenty-fifth. Stayed at the Jackson Inn, room one-seventy-five, until we came home on the twenty-seventh."

I cut my eyes toward Stewart once again. The smirk grew wider. I made a mental note to talk to him alone.

"How did you learn of your father's death?"

A tear formed in the corner of one eye. Despite her size, she looked vulnerable and frail. "When I got home from Jackson, the police were waiting for me. I was devastated."

Stewart shook his head and muttered a curse. "Roll up your pants. It's getting deep in here. I got to have a drink on that," he said, heading for the sideboard where the liquor was stocked. He reached for a bottle.

Annebelle's demeanor of vulnerability and frailty instantly metamorphosed into a rigid mask of case-hardened steel. She glared at him. "That shows you how much you know. You were glad to see him die. He told me about the fight you two almost had." She narrowed her eyes and clenched her teeth. "Yeah, and now that JW's dead, you can sell that drug den you call a beauty shop and take your boyfriend to live in New Orleans."

"Why you—" He slammed the bottle back on the side-board and in a fit of anger, charged across the room at her, drawing back his left arm. "I'll slap you silly!"

I grabbed him around the chest from behind, and using his forward momentum, slung him aside. He crashed into the Victorian couch, toppling it over backwards and sending him sprawling to the floor.

WR grabbed Annebelle just as she rushed toward her brother sprawled on the floor. "Stop it, stop it," he shouted, throwing his arms around her shoulders.

"He's not the only one who can play rough!" she screamed. "I'll show him!" She aimed a wild kick at Stewart that hit nothing but air.

Stewart stumbled to his feet. If I hadn't been standing directly in front of him, he would have charged her again. I held out my hand. "That's far enough. Cool off."

I could hear WR still struggling with Annebelle behind me, but I didn't dare take my eyes off Stewart, whose face was beet-red. The veins in his neck bulged. I hoped WR could hold her. Both of the combatants outweighed me. They'd flatten me flatter than the proverbial pancake if they caught me between them.

"Come on, Stewart," I said softly, nodding to the stairs in the foyer. "Let's go up on the gallery and cool off."

He hesitated, his brows knit and his eyes intense with hatred. After several tense moments, Stewart nodded briefly. I followed him up the winding stairs to the second-floor gallery just outside my bedroom. I had him alone.

To the west, the sun had dropped behind the hills of Vicksburg.

He half-sat, half-leaned against the railing and pulled out a pack of cigarettes. He offered me one. I shook my head. He grunted. "Wish I could stop," he muttered.

I remained silent.

After two or three puffs, he looked at me curiously. "WR said you talked to him. What about me? When were you planning on talking to me?"

With an indifferent shrug, I dropped into a weathered wicker chair against the wall. "I know just about all there is to know. The two of you were in Shreveport. The lawyer who called you didn't show."

"Yeah. A place called the Tiger's Den."

"How far is Shreveport? A couple hundred miles?"

"One eighty. I filled up when we arrived to see what kind of mileage I'm getting."

I didn't reply.

After several moments of silence, he cleared his throat. "What makes you think someone might have killed John?"

"Oh, different things. But, I could be wrong." A faint smile ticked up the edge of his lips, but quickly vanished when I added, "And I could be right. Take you for example."

He shifted his rear on the railing nervously. "What about me?"

"Well, I could make a good case against you. First, you don't have an alibi for the time your father died. Second, you have plenty motive. A split of twenty-three million dollars."

"I didn't know he was worth that much."

I rolled my eyes. "You know better than that, and that's my third reason. You see, Stewart, I know you put the land south of town on the market without your father's knowledge. If it wasn't valuable, why did you try to sell it?"

He glared at me a moment, then his belligerence melted before my eyes. "Yeah. I knew. The truth is, JW was hard-headed as a rock. I figured if he saw how valuable the land was, if he saw the number of offers we got, he might decide to sell it."

"Then why did WR tell Jack it was worthless?"

Stewart's cheeks turned red. He ducked his head. "We didn't want Jack or Annebelle to know just how valuable it was."

"Why not? If your father had given it to someone else, what good was all the lying and secrets?"

His cheeks grew redder. "We planned to contest the will."

I leaned back in the wicker and shook my head, disgusted with him and his brother. I cleared my throat. "According to what your sister just said, you and your father almost came to blows. Is that right?" I had two more pieces of evidence, but I didn't want to spring them too soon.

Stewart's pan-shaped face paled. Sweat ran down his jowls and dripped on his powder-blue blouse. "Yeah, but I wouldn't have hit the old man." He shook his head. "That old geezer could make me so mad I wanted to break his neck, but I would never have struck him."

That response gave me the opportunity to slip into my good guy routine. "I don't figure you would, just like I believe that you were surprised to learn your father left the land along the river to the four of you."

He grinned and nodded emphatically. "You can say that again. Sure, WR and me wanted the land. We, ah, we all have responsibilities. You know, debts, that sort of thing."

"Oh, I know, Stewart. I know your father gave you considerable sums of money. I know you owe the bank over a hundred thousand, and that you're behind in your payments. I know also that you have considerable gambling debts at the Riverboat Casino. Your father's death sure helped you out there, didn't it?"

His mouth dropped open. And then I hit him with fact number one that I knew he attended gay conventions in New Orleans, where he also had a lengthy arrest record, and his jaw hit the floor.

"How–how–how—"

I leaned forward in the wicker chair. "I have ways, Stewart."

He licked his lips and puffed nervously on his cigarette. "Well, I didn't kill him. It wasn't me."

"So some of what your sister said is true. With the inheritance, you are moving to New Orleans?"

"She's one to be talking. She hated John." He nodded to the parlor. "When she was in there saying how much his death devastated her, I could have puked. She hated his guts."

"Enough to kill him?"

Stewart hesitated, considering the question. Finally, he nodded sharply. "Yeah. Enough to kill him."

"Why? What happened between the two?"

"John wasn't much of a father. Mom died when Jack was five or six. John raised us. If he didn't like what one of us was doing, he'd grab the nearest belt or club and whale the daylights out of us. He was always worse on Annebelle. Not at first, but later."

"Why was that?"

He dropped his gaze to the floor. "When she was around thirteen or so, she stood up to him. He hated that, that one of his children should defy him. He slapped her, and that's why she ran away."

So far, his story followed the same lines as WR's account of the falling out between the two. "Where'd she go?"

"We had an aunt over in Jackson. She's dead now. Annebelle stayed there until Aunt Martha died, but then she had to come back here. Soon as she graduated from high school, she moved out. Been out ever since." He shook his head. "She sure has a temper."

I shook my head. "Well, from what I saw down there, you have one too."

His cheeks colored. "I lost it down there."

"A sharp prosecutor could make a point that you lost it with your father."

He looked at me, his brows knit. He held his temper. "Like I said, I didn't kill him—if it wasn't an accident."

"If I've seen it once, I've seen it a hundred times."

"What's that?"

"A good district attorney nailing the lid shut on some poor slob on a lot less evidence than you face."

He shook his head. "I don't care. I didn't do it."

"Normally, I'd probably believe you, Stewart. But this time . . ." I shook my head. "I don't know."

"What do you mean? Why can't you believe me?"

"Oh, I can believe it about you and WR going to Shreveport. And everyone goes into debt. But you know what really bothers me?"

"What?"

I played my last card, the evidence I'd been holding back. "The fact that you're the one who ordered the naphtha that exploded and killed your father."

Chapter Eighteen

Stewart stared at me in disbelief. "I what?"

"From information I uncovered, you ordered naphtha instead of the ACL cleaner John normally used." I arched an eyebrow. "You think some ambitious young prosecutor won't jump on the fact you ordered highly volatile naphtha instead of the much safer seven-seventy-Z Detergent?"

He pushed away from the rail and glared down at me, his rotund face growing livid. He sputtered, "That's a lie. I never ordered cleaning fluids for John. Who told you that?"

I remained seated and shook my head. "Never mind. When the time comes, you'll know."

"Look. I got a right to know." His tone took on a hard edge.

"Why, so you can confront the individual and give the district attorney another reason for suspecting you? For pete's sake, Stewart, use your head. Obviously, you haven't used it much in the last few years, but for your own sake, use it now. You, and your brother and sister—all three of you are already boiling in the cannibals' soup pot. Don't make the fire any hotter."

"It was Doc Raines, wasn't it? John always bought cleaning fluids from Doc. He's the one who told you, isn't he?" He glared at me.

I leaned back and grinned briefly. Then in an icy voice that belied the smile on my face, I said, "I promise you, Stewart. Harass the man, and I'll see you behind bars until this investigation is over. Hemings promised me that power." It was a lie, but Stewart had no way of knowing.

He glared at me for several seconds. Finally, his shoulders sagged, and he nodded. "Okay. But, what about Jack? Are you investigating him too?"

Leaning back, I steepled my fingers on my chest and rested my chin on them. I studied the floor as I spoke. "It's very possible, I suppose, that Jack could have rented an airplane, flown five hundred miles on the twenty-sixth, rented a car, drove out here, committed the deed, and returned." I nodded. "It's possible. But—" I looked up directly into his eyes. "But, not as possible or likely as one of you three." I pushed to my feet. "And trust me, Stewart, that's exactly how a prosecuting attorney will view it. "The three of you had motive, opportunity, and means. Jack's shy on opportunity and means."

Stewart sneered. "How do you know he didn't have the opportunity?"

"Because I was with him on the twenty-sixth."

He glowered at me. "Maybe you're in it with him."

All I could do was shake my head. "Grow up, Stewart. That's bull, and you know it."

Stewart grimaced and lowered his head. "Yeah."

I changed the subject. "You cooled off now?"

He grinned sheepishly. "I suppose."

"Good." I rose from the wicker. "I have some e-mail to get off. I'll see you downstairs," I said, opening the door to my bedroom. I wanted to run down the owner of the license plate I had memorized from the car carrier that helped run me off the road.

To my disgust, the site was down, scheduled to be open next morning at 8 A.M.

When I returned to the parlor, WR and Annebelle had left. "Got tired of arguing," Jack explained as he poured me a cup of coffee while he and Stewart sipped on glasses of bourbon. "How do you put up with all this, Stewart? I've only been here two days, and I'm ready to scream."

I couldn't help noticing that as the two brothers stood together, Jack was just a smaller image of Stewart, who was a head taller and fifty or sixty pounds heavier.

Stewart sipped his bourbon, and with a wry grin, replied, "I scream every night, little brother. Every night."

I chuckled to myself. I could believe that.

And I think I would have probably taken up screaming myself if I hadn't gotten out of that old house to pay a visit to Nancy Carleton, after which I planned to meet Diane down at the Golden Fleece Casino at the bottom of Clay Street.

Carleton lived in an apartment complex on Baldwin Ferry Road. Deeply tanned, she wore a green tank top, matching spandex shorts, and running shoes that looked like two clubs. A petite woman, she was an exact opposite of Annebelle Edney, even down to her short-cut black hair.

I explained the purpose of my visit. The smile on her face froze momentarily when she realized I was checking the veracity of Annebelle Edney's alibi, then beamed once again. She invited me in, but a look of wariness filled her eyes. "Something to drink? I have some sport drinks or water."

I declined. "I know it's late, Miss Carleton, but I won't keep you long. I just wanted to verify a couple things."

She nodded. "By all means."

"Annebelle Edney said you and she were in Jackson together this last weekend."

She nodded emphatically. "Oh, yes, Mr. Boudreaux. She

was there with our team. She was a tremendous help. She always is."

"Were there any times that she was out of your sight for a couple hours or so?"

She chewed on her bottom lip. "I don't really think so. Oh, there were times when we weren't playing that we scouted different games. But, I'd swear that I saw her every hour or so. I could be mistaken, but I don't think so."

"What about Saturday afternoon, around four. Were you playing a game then?"

"Let's see. No, we had a five-thirty game. We finished a game at one-thirty, and our next was at five-thirty."

"What did you do then? Scout other games?"

"Yes. Annebelle volunteered to scout the Monroe Marauders and the Beaumont Raiders. We figured we might be playing them in the next round." She laughed. "Waste of time. Both were eliminated before they got to us."

"I see, so you didn't see her from around one-thirty until five-thirty?"

Her brows knit in concentration. "I'd say about five-fifteen."

"Good enough, Miss Carleton. I appreciate your time."

She looked up at me, her eyes wide with surprise. "That's all?"

I smiled. "I'm a man of my word. I told you I wouldn't keep you long."

The steep hills of Vicksburg fascinated me. I was a flat-land boy until Mom and I moved to Austin, Texas, twenty or so years earlier, but I never could take the hilly country around Austin for granted. I had lived on the flat coastal Louisiana prairie too long.

As I headed down the steep slope of Clay Street, I realized I'd thought about Diane off and on throughout the day. I'd be lying if I denied seeing her had stirred some old familiar feelings as well as igniting a few flames of guilt over Janice.

As in most marriages that break up, Diane and I had just

drifted apart without realizing it until we were too set in our new roles to even make an effort to put the pieces back together.

I parked in the casino garage at the bottom of the precipitous hill and started across the street to the casino. Before stepping from the curb at the bottom of the hill, I looked up and down the darkened street. All clear. Halfway across the brick street, I heard the bump of tires and looked around to see the grill of a driverless Cadillac not twenty feet from me.

There was no time to think. I threw myself backward, hoping to escape the path of the runaway car. When I hit the ground, I kicked out with my feet against the bricks to shove me even farther from the path of the vehicle. Something struck the heel of my shoe.

In the next instant, I heard the shriek of ripping metal. I rolled over in time to see the Cadillac plow through a chain-link fence and carry a hundred feet of the galvanized net with it as it arched through the air and plummeted into the swirling waters of the Mississippi.

A hand touched my shoulder. "Hey, buddy. You all right?"

I looked up into the worried eyes of a young man in his early twenties. "Yeah. Yeah, I think so." I climbed to my feet.

He stepped back. "That was sure close. I didn't even see the Caddie coming until you jumped back. Are you sure you're all right?"

I brushed myself off. "Just a little shaken. But yeah, I'm fine."

By now, a crowd had gathered on the riverbank, peering into the river below. I walked past them to the casino.

We served ourselves on the casino buffet. I didn't mention my close call to Diane, but the fact that this was the fourth time someone had tried to run me off the case kept my mind preoccupied. At least it was until Diane said, "So, I hear you're in town to investigate JW Edney's death."

My fork froze at my lips. The runaway Cadillac instantly vanished from my thoughts. I stammered for a moment.

She smiled when she saw the confusion on my face. Flippantly, she explained, "Oh, everyone in town knows about it. I heard it from Jaybird—he's the one who owns the restaurant where we met last night. He heard it from some detective down at the police station." She wrinkled her forehead in concentration. "I don't remember his name."

Cursing under my breath, I lowered the fork. "Wouldn't be Tom Garrett, would it?"

"I'm not sure. The name sounds familiar."

My initial impulse was to rip out Tom Garrett's tongue, but then if I did that, Chief Hemings would probably throw me in jail and toss the key into the middle of the Mississippi.

Besides, I told myself, maybe it all works out for the best. Maybe I won't have to do as much legwork. I speared a chunk of broiled chicken and popped it in my mouth.

"Do you really think someone killed the old man?" She took a bite of a strawberry.

"Hard to say. There are several who could benefit from his death. The truth is," I added, hoping to change the subject, "I haven't had time to really dig into it." Before she could respond, I said, "Tell me about the Vicksburg Battlefield. Is it really worth seeing?"

For the remainder of our dinner, she regaled me with the history of the Siege of Vicksburg during the Civil War. "Come out during my shift, and I'll take you around. What about tomorrow?"

I was tempted but I had planned to check Annebelle's alibi at the Jackson Inn and speak with the coordinator of the softball tournament. "Depends. I've got to make a trip to Jackson in the morning. I'll call when I get back."

Back in my second-floor bedroom, I lay in the antique four-poster in the dark. With just a little imagination, the musty smell of the room, the patter of rain against the wood shake roof, and the feather mattress in which I sunk took me back to 1836 when this section of the house was built. Whoever had slept here must have heard the same sounds, smelled the same smells, and sunk as deeply into the feather mattress as I.

Chapter Nineteen

I awakened early, compiled my notes, grabbed breakfast on the go from McDonald's, and hit the interstate for Jackson. An hour later, I pulled into the parking lot of the Jackson Inn.

Many PIs use pretext when attempting to locate individuals. From time to time, I played various roles to accomplish the same trick, depending on the situation. I also learned that usually the most effective lever to gain information was by the generous exchange of money.

I grinned to myself when I spotted the young clerk behind the counter. Looked like a college kid. I played it straight, showing him my identification. "I'm checking to see if a certain individual spent the night of the twenty-fifth and sixth."

He frowned and glanced toward the office behind him. "I don't know if I can do that. Is that legal? I wouldn't want anything on my conscience," he added with a priggish arch of his eyebrows.

"I could get an court order, but that takes time." I pulled a twenty from my wallet and laid it on the counter. "This might help ease your conscience some. You don't have to say a word. Just look in that computer and see if Annebelle Edney and Nancy Carleton were here on the twenty-fifth and sixth. Room one-seventy-five."

He hesitated.

I pulled out another twenty.

The computer hummed. He studied the screen, then nodded. "They were here, at least Annebelle Edney was. Room one-seventy-five. Checked in at three-thirty-two in the afternoon on the twenty-fifth and checked out on the morning of the twenty-seventh at eleven-sixteen."

I thanked him, grinning to myself at just how simple it was to salve a guilty conscience. "One other question. The softball tournament that was in town. Who put it on? Any idea?"

He shook his head. "Sorry."

I headed to the Chamber of Commerce where I learned the city itself had sponsored the tournament. I represented myself as a civic-minded citizen from Austin, Texas, who had heard about the tremendous success of the tournament and was curious as to how the city had managed it. "Thirty teams," the city manager said with a broad grin. "Biggest turnout we've had in the five years we've been hosting it. We figure the tournament brought over two million dollars to the city."

"Whoever organized it must be pretty sharp."

"That he is. Matt Barnes. He's the athletic director for Jackson Public School District."

Matt Barnes was a tall, affable man with a mop of tangled gray hair sticking out from under his ball cap, and he was more than willing to discuss the details of the tournament. "We even videoed it using a digital sixteen millimeter camera and software," he said. "We edit it by team and then sell the videos or DVDs to team members and local citizens."

I couldn't believe my luck. Have you edited any yet?"

"You bet. We have a special unit from one of the local high schools for that. They start editing as soon as the first game ends."

"What about the team from Vicksburg? I have a friend over there who would love to have a copy."

"Sure. Video or DVD? Twenty bucks either one."

"DVD."

He went into another room and returned moments later with the disk.

"Is there anywhere I can preview it?"

He nodded to an open door behind him. "In my office."

I didn't need to look more than five seconds.

There, on the bench in the gray uniform of the Vicksburg Rebels sat, as she claimed, Annebelle Edney.

Annebelle was on my mind as I headed back to Vicksburg, driving at a modest sixty miles an hour. Her alibi held up. Still, I wasn't firmly convinced about her, although her reaction upon learning the true value of JW Edney's estate seemed to suggest she was as much in the dark of its true worth as Jack, or perhaps she was a better actor.

Of course, I reminded myself, I wasn't convinced about WR or Stewart either. Their only alibi was for each other, which was laughable.

I wasn't positive I had found the right motive or not. Sure, twenty-three million or so was motive enough, even shared among four children. I flexed my fingers about the steering wheel. Maybe I wasn't looking at it from the right perspective, but then, what other perspective was there with that much money at stake?

Could it be that one of them was so greedy, he or she wanted it all? That was hard to believe. On the other hand, given the hostility within the family, such a scenario wouldn't have surprised me.

"Just keep digging, Tony," I muttered. "Something will turn up."

And something did turn up, but not what I expected.

Where the pickup came from, I have no idea. I'm a cautious driver for the most part, always checking the rearview every thirty seconds or so. I glanced into the mirror. Behind me, the traffic on the interstate was sparse.

Ten seconds later, a blue pickup roared past. From the corner of my eye, I glimpsed a flash of fire. I looked around to see a Molotov cocktail, a bottle of gasoline with a burning torch in the neck, heading directly at my window.

All that saved me was that whoever hurled the Molotov cocktail must never have reached high school physics because he misjudged the speed of his pickup. But then most beef-witted dullards reduced to throwing Molotov cocktails don't even realize there is a relationship between speed and motion. They probably can't even spell either word.

Instinctively, I hit the brakes. The bottle struck the hood of my Silverado. My tires screamed in protest, but when I saw the explosive ricochet off the hood, I, in the vernacular of the eighteen-wheeler gearjammers, slammed the pedal to the metal.

By then the blue pickup was a quarter of a mile ahead. The powerful Vortec 5.3 V8 engine in my truck howled, and slowly I gained on him. I was almost close enough to catch the license number when another flaming cocktail came arching end over end from the truck. The bottle slammed on the interstate in front of me and exploded in a balloon of flame.

I slowed and swerved, and then there came another cocktail, followed moments later by a fourth. I cut my speed and swerved onto the shoulder to avoid the broken glass and flames strewn across the highway. By the time I slipped past the last fire, the blue pickup was but a dot on the horizon.

I studied the vanishing dot, wondering just how they knew I was in Jackson. I had told no one except Diane. I couldn't imagine her being mixed up in a plot to either run me out of town or kill me, but who else could have known?

Unless . . . maybe I'd been followed from the time I left Vicksburg, but if that was the case, why didn't they make the attempt on the way over?

I had no answers, so I did what any all-American boy would do—I decided to set up a sting for Diane.

By the time I reached the Vicksburg city limits, I had a two-part plan. Of course, the truth was, it wasn't much of a plan, but then I've never been too imaginative. Still, it was all I could come up with.

First, I called Diane and put off the tour of the battlefield. "I've got work to do at the house. If everything goes the way it should, I should know before morning if Edney's death was murder or an accident."

She sounded disappointed, and I wondered if I was right. If I was wrong, I would apologize, but if someone showed up that night, I'd know that it was Diane who passed on the word.

In addition, I planned to follow her when she left work. Perhaps she would lead me to whomever she had divulged my intentions. If that didn't work, maybe the second part would.

That was my plan. Simple. But then, I've always subscribed to the timeworn KISS principle: Keep it simple, stupid.

Chapter Twenty

Jack was out when I reached the old mansion.

My first job was to run down the license of the car carrier. The number was owned by Byrne Leasing Company in San Antonio.

Naturally, the company refused to divulge any information as to whom that carrier had been leased, so once again, I contracted the job to Eddie Dyson.

While waiting for Eddie's reply, I watched the DVD in my bedroom. Just as Annebelle had claimed, she was hitting practice balls, right-handed, to the infielders during warmup and sitting on the bench during the game.

I shook my head in disappointment, idly noting, but dismissing the fact there was an unusual number of southpaws on the team.

Naturally, for the remainder of the game, the few clips of her were mostly as teams switched places. I shook my head. A hundred-mile round trip in the span of three outs was too ludicrous a theory to entertain.

The team played two games Friday and two Saturday. Annebelle was on the bench in all of them.

Later that afternoon, I waited in a convenience store parking lot until Diane got off work. When she passed the parking lot, I slipped in behind her SUV, taking care to stay far enough to the rear so she wouldn't spot me. I hoped that sooner or later, she'd make contact with someone.

She didn't.

After stopping off at a Kroger's Supermarket on Pemberton Square Boulevard, she went straight to her apartment and remained inside. By ten o'clock, I'd had enough.

Upon returning to the house, I parked in front and stared through the windshield at the old mansion absently. My plan to tail Diane had failed. Now it was time to see if the second part worked.

Jack looked up when I entered. He was sprawled on the Victorian couch, his feet shamelessly resting on the ornate rosewood trim. He was working his artistry with the arm scratcher and watching some island reality program on TV. Leaving the plastic arm up his cast, he held up a tumbler of bourbon. His eyes were glazed, his fleshy cheeks flushed. "Hey, buddy. Good to see you. Help yourself."

I waved the offer away and poured a glass of water. "What have you been up to today?" I took a long drink.

He went back to working the scratcher, an expression of supreme ecstasy on his face. "Getting the estate ready for probate." He stroked faster. "I can't stop this blasted itch. What about you? Learn anything over in Jackson?"

I choked on the water. When I stopped coughing, I frowned at him. "Who told you about Jackson?"

"Stewart. Why? Was it some kind of secret?"

Trying to cover my surprise, I shrugged. "No. I just didn't expect you to know about it. No big secret. When did he come over?"

"He didn't. We met at the lawyer's with WR and Annebelle. I got there late. He mentioned it as we left."

"You mean just you and Stewart."

"Yeah."

I nodded, considering the information. Stewart and Diane? That didn't make sense. Not Stewart the gay blade.

"So," Jack said, breaking into my thoughts, "what was over in Jackson?"

"Waste of time," I replied, shaking my head. I headed for the stairs. "See you later. I've got some work upstairs."

He grunted and continued playing the fiddle with the scratcher. "I've got to see a doctor about this itching. There's bound to be something that'll help."

Upstairs, I sat at the ancient desk and made a pretense of fumbling through my note cards, all the while listening expectantly for the slightest sound outside on the gallery.

Nothing.

I strained to pick up sounds from the back stairs.

Still nothing.

Nagged by the feeling that I had missed something, that I had overlooked a small detail that could be important, I went back to my note cards.

At midnight, I rose and stretched my cramped limbs. So much for my plan to expose the killer. I growled, "Another bust." I headed for the gallery and some fresh air. Just as I stepped through the doorway to the gallery, a loud splat sounded in the door jamb at the side of my head. A thousand stinging pinpricks peppered my cheek.

Instinctively, I jerked aside and stumbled backward over the wicker chair. I hit the floor hard, banging my head against the cypress and heart pine boards. Stars exploded in my head. For a moment, I lay stunned, and then the pain hit the side of my face.

I grabbed at my cheek, but quickly jerked my hand away when a sharp object jabbed into my palm. "What the—"

Groggily, I rolled to my feet and staggered into my room. I still didn't know what had happened. I looked in the mirror in the adjoining bathroom. Blood ran down my cheek, which was pierced by several tiny slivers of wood.

Wincing, I gingerly picked them out, then soaped the

cheek thoroughly and washed it off. I rummaged through the medicine cabinet and found a bottle of alcohol, which I liberally doused on my still-bleeding cheek. The sting of the alcohol cleared the fog of pain in my head and shocked me into realizing just what had happened.

The noise, the flying slivers of wood meant only one thing. Someone had taken a shot at me.

Quickly, I turned off the lights. I pressed my handkerchief to my cheek, and, taking my time, I pulled the curtain back from the window jamb and peered into the night. I could see nothing in the thick vegetation below.

Using the darkness as cover, I headed for the rear stairs, feeling my way through inky blackness down the stairs, through the storage room, and into the dining room.

I peered around the edge of the dining room window. Even from this vantage point, I saw nothing in the Stygian darkness.

Minutes passed slowly, dragging into an hour. The only movement outside was the occasional cat slinking across the porch.

"Whoever it was is gone now," I muttered.

On impulse, I headed for my Silverado.

I drove past Stewart's apartment. His Cadillac was parked out front. Then I headed for WR's place. I was waiting at a red light at Pearl and Clay when Diane's red SUV sped past heading east. She was alone. "I wonder where she's going at this time of night?" I muttered. Without hesitation, I turned and followed.

At the end of Clay, she pulled into the parking lot of the Riverboat Casino. I braked to a halt at the curb across the street. I scooted down in the seat and peered over the bottom of the window. She parked and quickly scurried across the lot to a waiting Cadillac and jumped in.

Just as the Cadillac pulled out of the parking lot, another car turned in. Its headlights revealed the driver of the Cadillac. His plastered down black hair was easily recognizable. "Well, well, well, hello, WR, hello. Why am I not surprised to see you?" Pieces began to fit together, and they all involved Diane, WR and Stewart. Diane fed WR information, and he passed it along to Stewart.

I watched as the large car disappeared into the sparse, early-morning traffic. I remained staring after the vehicle, sorting my thoughts. I remembered that night in the bar with Diane. When I mentioned Jack Edney's name, she reacted. At the time, I thought it was simply the reflection of the jukebox in her eyes, but now, I realized it was recognition of Jack's surname, the same surname of the man whom it appeared she was dating.

Diane must have told WR or Stewart I was at the mansion tonight, and they sent someone to either frighten or kill me. She also must have told them I was going to Jackson, and he and Stewart sent the bombers after me.

Slowly, I drove back to the house, putting the plot together with two brothers and Goggins. The only way I could see it was that the three had conspired to write a new will.

Goggins had to be involved for he had received no follow-up letter after JW allegedly requested the new will on the sixteenth or seventeenth. And according to Wilson Jenkins and Doc Raines, JW Edney always wrote follow-up letters. I grinned wryly, silently thanking the Man Above for making JW Edney so eccentric.

It was a minor point, but one on which I thought I might be able to hang my theory. "So," I muttered more to myself than aloud, "who do you believe, Tony? JW Edney's fifty-odd-year habit or Goggins' version of the new will?

"Then, after JW died, they simply switched wills. Goggins was JW's lawyer. He had access, he had opportunity, and probably the brothers provided plenty of motive.

"Hold on," I added. "That doesn't work. If WR and Stewart wrote a new will, why did they put Annebelle in it?" The virulent animosity between brothers and sister was too intense, too palpable to simply be a mere charade.

I parked in front of the house and stared unseeing at the

shadows covering the old mansion, trying to find a logical answer to my last question.

No answer came. Disgusted, I opened the door and climbed out.

Next thing I knew, my head exploded, and I found myself falling into a bottomless pit.

Chapter Twenty-one

I don't know how long I fell, but heels digging into my stomach jarred me awake. I opened my eyes and discovered I was blindfolded and gagged. I tried to move a hand, but they were bound as were my feet.

A cruel laugh broke the silence. "Hey, Sal. The monkey's awake."

"Shut up, you big mouth." Sal then spoke to the driver. "How much farther we got to go?"

"Not far. Turnoff is just ahead."

My blood ran cold. I tried to move, but I was on the floorboard of the vehicle and my captors had their feet on me. I twisted my wrists.

"Stop squirming," one of them said. "You mess up the shine on my shoes, I'll really give you something to be sorry for."

If I hadn't been so scared, I might have laughed. *Something to be sorry for*? I had news for him. Right then I had all the sorry I could handle.

We turned off the highway onto a rough dirt road.

I'd often wondered how I would die. I hoped it would be in my own bed with my family around, not shot in the head and dumped out in the middle of nowhere.

The car jerked to a halt, backed up, and turned around.

"Okay, Manny. Get the bozo out."

Humid air filled with the swampy stench of decomposing animal and plant life rolled over me when they opened the door. Rough hands jerked me out and stood me up. I was blind and helpless, but I wasn't about to stay still for them. They were going to kill me, but at least I would be rolling on the ground in an effort to get away from them. A futile effort, but better than just standing and waiting for a slug.

Abruptly, the blindfold was yanked off my eyes.

The peripheral glow of the headlights showed a nattily dressed man about my age. The shadows cast by the snap-brim of his hat hid his eyes, but not the cruel smile on his thin lips. He shook his head. "You got no idea how lucky you are, you little monkey. Stop snooping. You've had enough warnings. Next time, you'll be feeding the 'gators."

"Can it, Manny. We're wasting time."

I glanced in the direction of the voice. My heart almost stopped when I recognized Sal Tonanno, supposedly a lieutenant in Joe Basco's mob in New Orleans. I looked away quickly, but myriad questions raced through my head. How was Basco involved, and who tipped him I was working the case?

Manny stared at me at moment longer, then following Tonanno, stepped into the limo and slammed the door.

The powerful car sped away, leaving me standing in the middle of a dirt road with a swamp on either side, my mouth, hands, and feet all duct-taped.

After the lights of the car disappeared, I looked around. Bullfrogs harrumped in a bassoon chorus from the darkness. Suddenly, off to my left, an alligator roared.

It is no understatement to say that bellowing roar got my attention instantly. I almost jumped out of my skin. Hastily, I ripped the gag from my mouth and stared at my bound hands. Sal and Manny had done a good job. My hands were taped together so that I couldn't move my fingers. Although I had a pocketknife, it wouldn't do me any good. But I had my teeth.

The alligator bellowed again, closer this time.

Frantically, I grabbed the tape with my teeth and began unwinding it, at the same taking short hops down the road away from the 'gator while casting anxious glances from the corner of my eyes at the dark swamp. Within ten or fifteen hops, I peeled the last of the tape away from my wrists, then hastily unwound the duct tape from around my ankles.

I glanced around. The stars provided a bluish-white light, enough to see the narrow road before me. In a trot, I headed in the direction the limo had disappeared, leaving behind my chorus of bullfrogs and alligators.

A mile or so down the winding road, I reached the highway and turned north. To the east, the sky was growing lighter as a false dawn crept toward me.

Ten minutes later, I caught a ride into Vicksburg.

Though I've rubbed shoulders with members of the mob while doing my job, I much prefer staying as far away from them as I can. And this last experience with them reinforced the wisdom of that predilection. On the other hand, I was curious as to what the mob had to do with whatever was going on with the Edneys.

Whatever it was, I figured I was close, otherwise, why the strong-arm stuff? What was on someone's agenda that would be profitable enough for Joe Basco's organization to take a hand? And what did Manny mean when he used the word 'warnings?' Was Basco behind the attempts on my life?

The sun was rising when I got back in my room. I paused before entering to examine the bullet hole in the door jamb. The slug hit the jamb near the inside edge, splintering it. Glancing over my shoulder into the thick undergrowth below, I wondered if the shooter was a bad shot or a very good one. Was this another attempt on my life or just a warning? And who was responsible? Basco? Or one of the Edney boys?

I probed the hole. The slug was deep, too deep to worry about now. I glanced around, studying the thick vegetation below.

I booted up my computer and accessed my mail. Out of the dozen or so e-mails, I spotted Eddie Dyson's. I opened the message. A few more pieces of the puzzle fell into place when I read that the car carrier had been leased to Rebel Trucking, the same company that owned the pickup driven by the construction worker who barely missed me with a bag of cement.

I planned to solicit Eddie to find out who owned Rebel Trucking, but, like the thorough little snitch he was, Eddie had already dug up the information. Rebel Trucking was a corporation, and one name of the three directors leaped out at me.

Joe Basco!

I had been right. He was behind the first two attempts on my life, maybe even the brick through my window and the Cadillac. I hesitated. Attempts? Maybe like Manny said, they were warnings. If Joe wanted me dead, I'd be feeding the alligators right now. So what was going on?

Staring out the window over the gallery, I wondered just how Basco got involved. The answer was obvious. He had to pick up the information from one of JW Edney's boys, either WR or Stewart. Other than Jack or Annebelle, no one else knew I was in Vicksburg that first day.

After I left for Doc Raines that first day, one of them could have called Basco, who then sent his boys to scare me off. But what did he have at stake?

Thoroughly puzzled, I shut down the laptop and placed a call to my high school pal, Danny O'Banion, Austin's resident mobster. There was a lot of talk, a lot of speculation about his connection with the Mafia, the Costa Nostra, the Mexican Mafia. That was the talk although nothing had ever been pinned on Danny. He had connections, and the truth is,

I knew some of them, but trust me, their names would never roll off my lips. That's how he wanted it, and as far as I was concerned, that's how I also wanted it.

Danny and I had a history going back to the eleventh grade when we scrambled through a few scrapes together. Then Danny left school before his senior year. Naturally, we drifted apart, but those months during our junior year bonded us. One year I ran into him at one of the annual football games between my alma mater, UT, and Oklahoma up in Dallas. We hit each other on the shoulder, lied a little, sipped from his silver flask a lot, and then went our separate ways.

Danny was inaccessible to most, but he always made an exception in my case because of our history.

"Hey, Tony. How you been doing? Long time no see."

We shot the breeze a few minutes, laughing over old times, reflecting on one of the times we worked together in solving a murder at the Chalk Hills Distillery out west of Austin.

"You must have a reason for the call, Tony." Danny laughed. "Or was it just that you missed my bubbling personality?"

I laughed with him. "No. I need to pick your brain, Danny. Joe Basco. You ever heard of him?"

The laughter fled his voice, replaced with a stiff wariness. "Why? Something going on?"

"No. Not with me. I don't want to have anything to do with Joe Basco."

He grunted. "Well, at least you're not as dumb as I thought. So what's up?"

"All I really want to know is if he has any plans up around Vicksburg, Mississippi?"

"Joe's got plans everywhere within five hundred miles of New Orleans."

I sensed Danny was trying to skirt my question. "So, he could have something going on around Vicksburg?"

Danny hesitated. "Yeah. I suppose he could."

The circle Danny was taking me in was growing larger

and larger. I decided to take him into my confidence. "Look, Danny. I know he is involved with a family named Edney in Vicksburg. The old man is dead. They say it was an accident, but I have evidence that makes me think it was not an accident."

"Careful, Tony. Basco don't take to being accused of murder."

"I'm not accusing him or his boys. I think one of the Edneys did it. If Joe's dealing with any of them, it could rub off on him if I'm right."

Danny remained silent for several moments. Suspicion edged his voice when he replied. "Why are you looking out for Basco?"

I didn't want to string out the story about the cement and Eddie Dyson's information, so I simply replied, "Long story, but to make it short, I just got back from a ride with a couple of his boys, Sal Tonanno and one called Manny. They left no doubt in my mind what would happen if I continued my investigation." I forced a weak attempt at a laugh. "And to be perfectly candid, I'm not particularly fond of the idea they suggested, so I want Joe to know that I'm working for him, not against him. Whatever he has going on around Vicksburg is not part of what I'm looking for. I'm just trying to find out who killed JW Edney."

"How'd you come to know Sal Tonanno?"

"I don't. I recognized him from his picture on TV."

Danny remained silent once again. "Okay. I won't guarantee nothing, but I'll get word to Joe."

"Right away, Danny?"

"Yeah, pal. Soon as we hang up."

"Thanks. I owe you."

"Take me to dinner when you get back. I'm hungry for a good barbecue."

Danny worked fast, and Joe Basco worked fast.

After I showered and shaved, I took a short nap. When I

left the house at noon, I found my friends from the night before parked beside my Silverado. The rear window hissed down and Sal Tonanno looked up at me. In a cold, matter-of-fact voice, he said, "Mr. Basco says if you queer his deal, you're a dead man."

"What deal?"

He didn't reply. The window started up.

"Listen, I've got to know just how far I can go, or what I can't touch. What deal?"

The window closed, but the car didn't move. Moments later, the window hissed back down. Tonanno stared up at me. "Mr. Basco plans to build a casino south of Vicksburg on the new highway."

I gulped, but managed a jerky nod, and watched as the limo pulled away.

Two or three pieces of the puzzle popped together, but not the way I would have chosen. If Basco was planning to build a casino, he had to have land. Was it possible he was interested in the Edney land south of Vicksburg, land through which the government was planning on constructing a new interstate?

That made sense to me. A thousand acres were more than enough for a sprawling complex of casinos, hotels, restaurants, fueling stations, and various other attendant businesses.

A chill ran up my spine. What would Basco do to me if my theory was right? If my theory was true, the will would be invalid. Abigail Collins and the Madison Parish Ornithological Society would have their bird sanctuary, and Joe Basco would not have his coveted casino.

I whistled softly, doubting very seriously if Joe Basco would appreciate the ecological benefit that a bird sanctuary would provide to that part of the state as much as he would a new gambling casino.

For a few worried moments, I questioned the wisdom of continuing the investigation now that Basco was involved. Still, there was Jack. Besides, I told myself in an effort to put a little stiffener in my backbone, you can't tell how the cards will fall until the hand is dealt.

Then another thought hit me. Why would Stewart and WR put the land on the market if they had a deal set up with Basco?

Were they trying to mislead someone? And if so, who? Or were they, as Stewart had admitted, simply trying to get JW to see the value of the property?

I took a deep breath and released it. I hated leaving unanswered questions behind because they could come back to haunt me. Of course there was always the chance I would find the answer down the road.

Now, I figured my next step was to find out which of the Edneys conspired with Goggins to change the will. At first, I had figured Stewart since he was the one who commissioned Bayou Realty to sell the property.

But now with WR in the picture, either brother could have sent the bombers and the shooter after me, and put Basco on my tail. No way I could see one of them implicated without the other.

Goggins, I had nailed. There was no wisdom in questioning him any further. The wrong word could make him suspicious.

Absently, I wandered toward the burned-out hull of the workshop while I reprised my theory in my head. Stewart and WR had somehow contacted Basco about the land; then altered the will; murdered the old man; and finally after probate, planned to pocket his share of $23 million, maybe more.

A neat little plot.

Now all I had to do was prove it.

I decided to start with Dorene Edney, three-time ex-wife of WR Edney.

Chapter Twenty-two

Dorene Edney lived on Mission Street. A petite woman in her early fifties, she stood around five-two and maybe a hundred pounds. Model-thin, she was stylishly dressed in black pedal pushers and a puffy white blouse with the collar turned up. Her brown hair made her look as if she had just stepped out of a beauty salon. But beneath the carefully applied makeup, she was hard.

Her black eyes studied me suspiciously as I explained the purpose of my visit. When I concluded, she scrutinized me another moment or so, then invited me in. She led the way into the living room, indicating an upholstered chair across the coffee table from the couch. "There isn't much I don't know about that man," she said, folding a leg under her as she lowered herself onto the couch. "We're divorced." She smiled wryly. "For the third time."

"I know. WR told me."

"So, you think he killed John?"

I had to admire her bluntness. A straight-to-the-point woman. "I don't know, Mrs. Edney. All—"

"Ms.," she said, interrupting.

"Sorry. Ms. Edney. Like I was saying, I know he owes the bank almost a quarter of a million, and he tried to talk his father into selling the land. Do you think he's capable of killing his father?"

She reached for a cigarette and held it up to me, her gesture asking me if I minded. I shook my head. She lit it, and in a chilling tone replied, "In a heartbeat. All WR cares about is money. He'd go to any lengths for a buck."

"Did he ever hint at anything like that while you were married?"

Her reply disappointed me. "No. In all fairness to the jerk," she replied, shaking her head. "Nothing like that." She inhaled deeply and blew out a stream of smoke toward the ceiling. "How much did John leave WR?"

"The four will split around twenty, maybe twenty-three million."

She raised her eyebrows. I could see the calculator humming. "That's around six million each."

"Yeah." I chuckled. "Before taxes. Afterward, maybe four."

Dorene Edney shook her head. "It won't last WR long. That man has a knack for bad investments. That's why he's in the hole he's in now."

"What kind of investments?"

With a weary shrug, she said, "Oh, the typical. Stock market, fly-by-night schemes, you name it. He's tried them all, looking for the pot of gold. He never did find it."

"What about Stewart and Annebelle?"

She looked me directly in the eye. "The whole family is messed up, Mr. Boudreaux. Nothing any of those people would do could surprise me. There was never a holiday, never a family get-together that wasn't ruined by a fight. And I'll tell you something else. John Wesley Edney might have given the appearance of a holy Christian, but he stirred up as much trouble as the kids. The one I felt sorry for was Annebelle. You knew she had gone to live with an aunt."

"Yeah. They told me."

With a sigh of frustration, she continued. "Then the aunt

died. That was a bad break for Annebelle because she had to move back in with John and the boys."

"What was so bad about that?" I remembered WR and Stewart's explanation. I was curious about Dorene's.

"She had to stand against the three of them. Those men acted like she didn't exist. It was a man's house, man's interest. Hunting, fishing, cars—I doubt if John ever hugged his daughter, much less told her he loved her. As soon as she graduated from high school, she moved out." She gave a terse grunt. "I imagine Stewart and WR were surprised the old man included her in the will."

If you only knew how much. "I guess you could say that," I replied simply.

Using the cigarette she held between two extended fingers as a pointer, she gestured to the neat little bungalow around her. A single tear formed in the corner of one eye. "This isn't much, but even the cheapest piece of furniture in this room is worth more to me than that family. You want to know how bad it really was? It was so bad that even the six million is not enough to persuade me to attempt a reconciliation with WR."

I remained silent.

Tears gathered in her eyes. "The truth is I really loved him at first. I wanted to be a part of him, but he kept pushing me away. As an innocent young girl, I'd always been taught that marriage was a blending of two souls into a single spirit stronger than either. Not WR. He believed a woman was put on this earth for man's comfort, pleasure, a clean house, and dinner on time." She took a deep drag of her cigarette and laughed bitterly. "By the time the third divorce rolled around, I was just as distant and callous as WR." She arched an eyebrow. "Constant rejection will make you a hard, unfeeling person, Mr. Boudreaux. Did you know that?"

I had the strangest feeling that she had managed to peer deep into my soul. "Yes, ma,am. That's what I've heard."

* * *

Later, I sat in my truck studying the small bungalow, going over our conversation in my head. I couldn't help feeling sorry for her. And I couldn't help thinking about Janice and me. Was that what I was doing now, rejecting her? Was what I considered a desire for control simply her effort to build a single spirit stronger than either of us? Had I created the problem in my own mind?

I pushed the thoughts aside and started the engine. I couldn't believe that in these last few days I still had come up with nothing more than enough loose ends to fill the Astrodome.

Chapter Twenty-three

As I waited at the signal light on the corner of Mission and Clay, a black limousine sped past. It was either the one in which I had been taken for a ride, or its twin. And if I was right, Sal and Manny were inside. On impulse, I followed, taking care to remain several car lengths behind. I had a sneaky feeling of their destination.

I was right. The limo pulled into the crowded parking lot of the Riverboat Casino and turned into a private parking area on the north side.

"What do you know," I muttered, quickly parking and hurrying into the casino.

Inside, the noise level was only a couple of decibels below that of a jet engine. Gaudy lights shone on plush red carpets, reflecting off the silver and glass of the slots. Bells and whistles from the whirling machines echoed off the high ceilings, and excited voices from the tables punched holes through clamor so thick that not even the proverbial hot knife could cut it. I paused to study the layout of the casino. I didn't figure Sal and Manny came in to play the slots or tables. Joe Basco probably had an interest in the casino. I wandered through the slots while covertly searching the spacious casino for the administrative offices.

Then I spotted the door to the offices beside the coin

exchange windows. I found a slot machine and started dropping quarters in it. Five minutes and twenty dollars later, the door opened and Sal and Manny strode toward me. I turned my back as they passed.

I studied the door from which they had come, convinced now more than ever that both Stewart and WR were in the scheme together. Both brothers were deep in debt, both to the bank, and Stewart also to the Riverboat Casino, a.k.a. Joe Basco.

I now believed more than ever that to cover their debts, the brothers conspired with lawyer Goggins to change the will; work out a deal with Basco for the land; and who knows, maybe even have their father killed by one of Basco's thugs.

Still, I reminded myself, there was one big problem with my theory. Annebelle. If the brothers orchestrated the plot, why include her in the will? Could it be a cunning effort to remove themselves from the sphere of blame? Were they that smart? Was Goggins that smart?

At that moment, the office door opened, and Stewart Edney stepped onto the floor. I ducked behind a slot.

I followed Stewart to the glass door at the entrance to the casino and watched as he climbed in his Cadillac and sped away.

Nodding slowly, I guessed I had finally stumbled across information to indicate I was heading in the right direction. It was time to check Stewart's alibi, his and WR's. I glanced at my watch. Three o'clock. If I hurried I could be back in town by nine.

Swinging by the house, I picked up pictures of the Edney family. Jack frowned. "What do you want them for?"

Slipping the pictures in my shirt pocket, I replied, "I'll explain later. See you about nine or ten."

I headed for Shreveport, a hundred and eighty miles to the west. The speed limit was seventy. I stayed at seventy-five, yet for every car I passed, a dozen passed me.

I reached the Tiger's Den at 6:15. Like most bars, the interior was lit by peripheral illumination cast by multi-hued lights from the jukebox and from behind a valance above the bar. Behind the bar was an artistic rendering of a crouching tiger. Unfortunately, the artist had a problem with perspective because the snarl on the animal's lips looked more like a sappy grin, and his back legs both came out of the same socket.

I ordered a draft beer and showed the pictures to the bartender. I indicated WR and Stewart. "You ever see these guys? Somebody said they were in here last Saturday."

He eyed me warily. "You a cop?"

"Nope. Private investigator. Long lost sons. Inherited several million dollars. I'm trying to find them for the family." It was a ridiculous story, but he took it.

He gave me a crooked grin. "The one on the left looks like me."

I laughed. "Sorry, pal. What about it? You see them?"

He shook his head. "Can't help you, sorry."

"You sure?"

"Positive. I just started work here yesterday. Let me call Jumbo."

"Jumbo?"

"Yeah, the owner. Hold on a minute."

Moments later, Jumbo, an apt nickname for he was a good six inches over my five-ten and a hundred pounds beyond my one-eighty, lumbered up to the bar. His meaty hand engulfed mine. I showed him the pictures. "Ain't seen them." He paused, frowned. "When was they supposed to be here?"

"Last Saturday."

He snorted. "Somebody's lying to you, boy. We was closed last Saturday. Cops busted us for selling to minors. We just opened back up Monday."

For a moment, I stared at him without comprehending his words. Then they hit me, right between the eyes. My first real break! I suppressed my elation. Jumbo had blown WR's and Stewart's alibis out of the water. If they had not been at the Tiger's Den, just where had they been? In the workshop with John Wesley Edney? That's how it now appeared.

During the drive back to Vicksburg, I enumerated aloud the chain of evidence I had gathered so far. "First, WR and Stewart owe the bank out the kazoo. Second, Stewart has gambling debts at the Riverboat Casino, which Joe Basco either owns outright or is a partner. Third, the mob boss wants to buy the Edney land south of Vicksburg. Fourth, I saw Stewart coming out of the casino offices. Fifth, Diane told WR I was going to Jackson, so he sent the bombers; sixth, Basco has an interest in Rebel Trucking, vehicles involved in two attempts on my life; and finally the two brothers had no alibi for the twenty-sixth just like Annebelle had said."

The last remark about Annebelle had sprung unconsciously from my lips. I frowned, trying to remember when she had made it. I pulled the three-by-five cards from my pocket and spread them on the seat. With one eye on the highway and the other on the cards, I shuffled through them, but could find no mention of the incident.

I struggled to remember. Slowly, it came to me. "Yeah. Yeah, that second night when Stewart had questioned her about softball, and she remarked that 'at least I have an alibi.'"

I frowned. How could she have known they had no alibi unless she was part of the plot with WR and Stewart? I jotted the question on a card.

As I now saw it, with the testimony of Wilson Jenkins and Doc Raines, and if I could tie one or both of the brothers to the attorney, William Goggins, I should have enough proof to convince Chief Hemings that JW Edney had been murdered.

Pretty solid, but yet, in the back of my head, I still had that nagging feeling that I was overlooking something.

Just as I reached the Mississippi River, a drizzle began to fall. "I don't believe it. Rain again." By the time I pulled up in front of the old mansion, the clouds had opened up.

Chapter Twenty-four

When I returned, I found that Diane had left a phone message for me. I gave her a call.

"Hi," she said cheerily when she picked up the receiver. "I know it's late, but I was wondering if you would like to grab something to eat."

Instantly, I grew wary but I kept my voice amiable. "Sure. What's the occasion?"

"Nothing important. I heard you were still in town, so I figured to show you some Vicksburg hospitality."

"Sounds good to me. Where?"

"What about Casper's Steak and Shrimp House, where I work part-time? I'll meet you there."

I couldn't believe my luck. Here was the perfect opportunity to lay a trap for WR and Stewart. "Fine with me. I'll be right over. Ten minutes."

Hastily, I put together a scheme to draw the brothers out. I regretted I didn't have more time to lay my plans thoroughly because unfortunately, when I worked too fast, I had a history of mistakes. "But," I muttered, quoting a hokey phrase I had heard somewhere, "time and tide wait for no man."

I planned to casually reveal to Diane that I had a solid contact with irrefutable evidence of conspiracy in the death

138

of JW Edney. I was planning on meeting him later that night. With luck, someone who didn't want the meeting to take place would get the word and show up.

Now the truth was, I had an aversion to any sort of physical confrontation. So if someone did show, I planned to surreptitiously fit a bumper bug on his car and then follow from a safe distance.

As an afterthought, I locked my .38 in the glove compartment.

Just before I reached the steakhouse, I remembered the battlefield from the brochure I had skimmed my first night at the motel. The only sites I could recollect were the Illinois Memorial and the Shirley house a couple of hundred yards east of the memorial on the crest of the same ridge. That would have to do for a meeting place.

I had to admit, Diane was a knockout that night. Her shiny brown hair fell down on her bare shoulders. She wore a yellow sundress that provided a becoming contrast to her tanned skin. And I couldn't help noticing she wore my favorite perfume. She had pulled out all the stops. A Cajun Mata Hari.

During the meal, we made idle conversation. Afterward, we retired to the bar where she ordered a cocktail, and I availed myself of club soda with a slice of lime.

"Well," she said jauntily, "how's the investigation going? When I heard you were still in town, I guessed you didn't have any luck the other night."

With a shrug, I replied, "Way it goes. Sometimes things work out, sometimes they don't. But, let's not talk about that. How's your family, your mom and dad? I haven't seen them for years."

She failed to cover the flicker of impatience that wrinkled her forehead. "Why they're just fine. What about your mom?"

For the next several minutes, we made small talk, but I could sense her impatience. She was dying to question me about the investigation.

I gave her the opportunity as we danced around the stamp-sized dance floor. "Hope you don't mind if we leave in thirty minutes or so."

Her body stiffened slightly against mine, but she kept her cheek against my shoulder. "Oh?" She tried to sound casual.

"Yeah. I'm supposed to meet a man tonight. He says he knows who killed the old man, and he also has proof the will was a forgery." Hoping I had not been too obvious, I waited for her response.

She struggled to keep the excitement from her voice. "A forgery?"

I nodded.

"Do you think he really does?"

"Who knows?" I suppressed a grin. She had taken the bait. I tightened the line gradually. "The only constant in this business is that you never know what will happen next." I gave another gentle tug on the fishing line. "If you hadn't called me, I would have called you."

"Oh? Why is that?" Her obvious puzzlement appeared genuine.

"This guy wants to meet at the battlefield tonight. Someplace out there called the Illinois Memorial. Supposed to be near the Shirley house. You know the place?"

She pulled back and looked up into my eyes. She studied me a moment. "Yes. Sure."

"Can you tell me how to get there?"

"You can't," she replied, shaking her head. "The park is closed at night. Only security is out there."

It was my turn to look into her eyes. "But I've got to. It might only be a wild goose chase, or it could be my only chance to break the case wide open." I paused a moment, then squeezed her hand. "Come on. Tell me where it is."

She pulled away from me, and taking my hand, led me back to the table. "I shouldn't," she said, glancing around the noisy bar. "But I want to help you. For old time's sake."

If she hadn't been looking at me, I would have rolled my eyes.

She continued. "Here, let me show you." She quickly drew the tortuous route from the park entrance to the Illinois Memorial where she placed an X. "Here it is." To the right, she drew another X. "This is the Shirley house. The memorial is to the west, about a hundred yards from the house. They're both on the same ridge." She drew an imaginary line from the house to the memorial. "The road dead ends another two or three hundred yards farther west at the Louisiana Redan."

I nodded. "Okay. But, if the park is closed, how do I get in?"

She smiled wickedly. "Like the teenage parkers do, drive across the grass."

"What about security?"

Her voice dropped to a whisper. I leaned across the table to hear her. "Two units. One from either direction." She glanced at her watch. "What time are you meeting him?"

"One o'clock."

"It's eleven now. Between twelve-thirty and one-thirty, each unit takes a thirty-minute lunch break. That means only one unit is out. That's your best chance of slipping in without being spotted."

I indicated the location of the Illinois Memorial on the map she had drawn. "It looks like there is only a single road. What about someplace to hide my truck when security passes?"

She pointed to the Illinois Memorial. "A drive goes around in back. You can hide your pickup there."

I laid my hand on hers and squeezed. "Thanks, Diane. I don't know what I would have done without you." Despite knowing that as soon as I left, she would run to WR, I still felt like the hypocrite.

With a deep sigh, I pushed the feeling aside. What had been between us was dead, relegated to the dark storeroom of disappointed memories.

Chapter Twenty-five

When I left the steakhouse, the rain had momentarily ceased, and a full moon shone over Vicksburg through patchy clouds. I pulled into a convenience store and purchased a map of the battlefield and its sites. The sixteen-mile route formed a tortuous circle, twisting and snaking over and around the tree-covered hills. The exit to the park was a hundred yards west of the entrance, the spot from which Diane had drawn her map.

I parked across the street and waited.

Sure enough, at exactly 12:30, one security unit pulled up to the Visitors' Center and two park officers went inside just as the second unit set off from the exit, making its way around the route in reverse.

With headlights off, I waited for a gap in the traffic on Clay Street, then shot across the road, eased over the curb, and raced across the grass. I glanced at the Visitors' Center, hoping neither of the park officers was peering from the window.

Fortunately, the full moon lit the road, making driving without lights a snap except for under the giant oaks and pecans spreading their ancient limbs across the battlefield.

Ten minutes later, I spotted the Shirley house, and beyond, the dome of the Illinois Memorial glistening in the

142

moonlight. I stopped at the intersection by the house. The road continued west to the dead end Diane had mentioned. The park route itself turned north.

I had no intention of hiding my truck behind the Illinois Memorial as Diane suggested. It was an obvious trap. Instead, I turned north. A broad grin jumped on my face because just beyond the Shirley house, a dirt road led back into the forest.

After parking, I hesitated, staring at the locked glove compartment in which lay my .38. For a moment, I toyed with the comforting idea of taking it with me, but I remembered Hemings' warning, and I didn't want to end up in a Mississippi jail.

Hopping out, I opened the toolbox and removed my black satchel from which I took a bumper bug, a flashlight, and the roll of duct tape.

I clambered up the muddy hill through the darkness to the rear of the house. Even in the light of the full moon, it didn't take a professional carpenter to see that the house was in a sad state of repair.

Remaining in the shadows of the house, I studied the Illinois Memorial to the west, the moon bathing the white dome in stark relief. As Diane said, both the house and the memorial—which was modeled after the Roman Pantheon—were located on a ridge about fifty feet high, the crest of which stretched over a hundred feet in breadth.

I hurried along the crest of the ridge to the memorial where I taped the flashlight to the open doors, pointing down.

Quickly, I hurried down the forty-seven granite steps leading up to the portico of the memorial and hid in the shrubs across the drive.

My plan was simple. If WR or Stewart did send someone, they'd have to climb the stairs to the beam of light. That would give me time to slip across the drive, place the bug under the bumper, and vanish back into the shrubbery.

Then I could follow them.

* * *

The clouds began to gather. Thirty minutes later, the drizzle started once again. I muttered a curse. All I could do was stay where I was, huddled behind the shrubs, feeling sorry for myself.

Time dragged.

Soon, the drizzle tapered off, and the cloud cover drifted slowly northward.

When I heard the faint crunch of gravel, I forgot all about my discomfort. I peered down the road and spotted the black silhouette of a pickup easing around a curve, heading directly for the memorial.

My heart thudded against my chest. I wished I had acted against my better judgment and slipped the .38 in my pocket. Still, if my plan worked, I would have no need for heat.

Abruptly, the dark truck stopped, still a hundred yards away. The doors remained closed.

Muttering to myself, I eased through the underbrush toward the vehicle. I dropped to my knees when the door swung open. The interior remained dark. A figure stepped out and looked around. "There's a light up there. I'll slip up there and take care of them." I stiffened when he added, "He won't get away this time like he did from the Caddie."

The speaker was a black silhouette against the lighter background of the steep ridge. He headed for the memorial. After he passed me, I eased forward, keeping the row of shrubs between the pickup and me. I was counting on the driver's attention to remain on his partner.

Quickly, I placed the bug, then headed up the ridge to my pickup. I couldn't afford to fall too far behind them when they left, or I couldn't pick up the bug.

Halfway up the ridge, a beam of light framed me. I froze. "Hey," a voice shouted from the memorial, "there he is!"

Down below, the pickup door slammed shut. Galvanized into action, I raced to the top of the ridge. Bobbing up and down, the beam of light from the memorial headed in my direction. The second man was still a hundred yards below. I kept waiting for someone to start shooting as I reached the crest where I stumbled and tumbled head over heels down the backside.

The first man took an angle to cut me off from the thick woods, but I reached the edge of the forest well ahead of him. I raced down a well-used trail, which, only a few feet into the thick woods, turned out to be darker than the inside of a cow. Quickly, I hid behind an ancient oak—and waited.

The beam of light bounced up and down as it drew closer. Then I could hear the footsteps. I said a fast prayer hoping that my timing wasn't too far off. Just as my pursuer reached the oak behind which I had hidden, I stepped out and threw a right hook, catching him squarely on the forehead and slamming him to the ground. He hit hard. I grabbed his flashlight and raced through the woods for my truck, shaking my stinging fist. I could hear their grunts as they raced after me.

"Shine the light over here," one shouted. "He got my flashlight."

"Hurry up. We got to get the guy. I don't want Jumbo mad at me like he was at those truckers."

I almost slid to a halt in surprise. Jumbo! Did I hear right? Jumbo? Truckers?

Then came a sickening thump and a sharp scream. Then all I heard was one set of footsteps. I grinned. Somebody had straddled a tree in the darkness.

Moments later, I jumped in the Silverado and slammed it into reverse. Through the windshield, I saw a single light bobbing up and down, coming in my direction. I gunned the engine. The ground was muddy from the rain, and the rear wheels slid off the drive. The rear bumper slammed into a tree with a crunch. My head snapped back, then popped forward.

The light was drawing closer.

I shifted into drive and eased forward several feet, then yanked it into reverse.

Suddenly, an orange spurt of fire erupted beside the flashlight followed by the splat of a slug hitting the windshield. I concentrated on the narrow drive in my side mirror. I figured I had less than thirty seconds to back out before he was on me.

I've had some unnerving experiences, and concentrating on backing out of a muddy, winding driveway with someone taking potshots at me ranks right up there.

But I made it. I reached the road and promptly made my next mistake. I took the long route out of the park instead of backtracking over the shorter one.

By now, the light southerly breeze had swept the clouds from the sky once again, leaving behind a glittering overhead of stars against a sky of black velvet. I flipped on my headlights as I raced around the circuitous route, hoping to reach the exit far enough ahead of my pursuers so I could hide until they passed. Then I could follow the bug I'd placed on their bumper.

That wasn't to be.

Within minutes, headlights popped into my rearview mirror. A cold chill ran down my back when I spotted the telltale orange mushrooms of fire from the passenger's window. They were shooting at me.

I took the curves as fast as I dared. What few stretches that permitted fifty or sixty miles an hour abruptly ended in switchbacks that would roll a vehicle at thirty.

A few miles farther, I cut right. The pickup stayed on my tail. I passed a road on the left, and to my surprise, the truck behind slid to a halt in the middle of that road.

I glanced in the rearview mirror. "I don't know why you stopped, buddy, but I ain't stopping," I muttered between clenched teeth. Seconds later, I saw why he had stopped. The road I was on made a giant circle right back to the parked pickup.

So, I did what anyone would do. I pulled up on the opposite side of the circle from them. And waited. On a rise between us was a statue of Ulysses S. Grant mounted on his steed. I glanced at my glove box. To heck with Hemings, I said to myself, removing the keys from the ignition and unlocking the compartment. The heft of the .38 in my hand felt reassuring. I restarted the engine.

If they came one way, I'd go the other. I smirked. I had them now. Abruptly, my smirk vanished. I squinted into the starlit night, and all I could do was mutter a soft curse.

Leaving their pickup to block the intersection, one headed down the middle of the road coming up from behind while the other came down the middle of the road ahead of me. Taking a deep breath, I rolled down the window and, .38 in hand, I rested my left arm on the side mirror. I cocked the .38 and muttered through clenched teeth. "Well, boys. If that's how you want to play the game, let's get at it."

With that, I floored the accelerator and sent the truck hurtling toward the figure in front of me. My headlights picked him up. When he realized my intention, he spread his legs in a firing position and brought up both arms. Before he could get in position to fire, I triggered off three shots.

There was no way I could hit him with the truck bouncing one way and me bouncing another, but three bursts of gunfire and a two-thousand-pound truck bearing down on anyone except Godzilla were enough to send him leaping from my path. He sprawled on the ground. I roared past, aiming for the narrow space between the rear of his pickup and the curb.

I dropped the .38 beside me on the seat and grabbed the wheel with both hands as I bounced the right tires over the curb—one set of wheels was on the street, and one set was off. I clenched my teeth, waiting for the impact, but I swept past the rear of his pickup with one coat of paint to spare.

"Now, let's get out here," I muttered.

Give the devil his due. Those two gorillas were persistent.

The next couple of miles, there were stretches where I hit eighty, but always at the end loomed that ever-present switchback. Another mile or so, the route straightened once again and by that time, the pickup was tailgating me. I glanced in the rearview and mumbled between clenched teeth. "I don't know who you are, pal, but you can drive."

Having no luck with their hardware, they decided to run me off the road. Just after I slid around the sharp curve at Stockade Redan, the pickup pulled up and slammed into me. Metal shrieked. I whipped the wheel back to the right, bouncing them over the curb.

Seconds later, they bounced me over the curb on my side. For the next mile or so, we jockeyed for position at eighty miles an hour, taking turns knocking each other back and forth. I had just slammed into him when suddenly, a bridge popped up directly ahead.

I stomped on the brakes as he swerved sharply toward me, only I wasn't there to stop him. He hurtled across the road, jumped the curb, ripped through a chain-link guard fence, and arched through the air a hundred feet to the road below. The pickup exploded into flames on impact.

Without hesitation, I sped away. Beyond the bridge, I pulled off the road into the trees and waited. Sure enough, moments later, a security unit sped past. When it was out of sight around a curve, I raced for the exit, hoping I could slip out of the park before the fire trucks and police arrived. I'd really have some trouble explaining all that had taken place.

Back at Jack's, I surveyed the damage to my Silverado. I cursed when I saw the mangled metal. I cringed when I found three bullet holes in my tailgate and another in my windshield. This trip to Vicksburg was becoming expensive. It was a good thing Jack was going to be a millionaire.

I grimaced when I thought of the fate of Jumbo's two thugs. I'd never know their identity. All I knew was they worked for Jumbo of the Tiger's Den in Shreveport and that Jumbo had something to do with Rebel Trucking. Was Jumbo working for Basco, who was on the board of the trucking firm? That appeared to be the next logical step in my little theory.

Chapter Twenty-six

I lay in bed wide awake, staring into the darkness and trying to make sense of the peculiar twist the case had taken. Even though I could not reconcile Annebelle's inclusion in the bogus will, I had been ninety percent convinced that WR and Stewart conspired to murder their father and somehow persuade Goggins to change the will and forge the old man's signature.

But now, Jumbo stepped into the picture. If he and Basco were in the scheme with the two brothers, why would he deny seeing WR and Stewart at the Tiger's Den? He could have provided them with the proverbial ironclad alibi.

Was he double-crossing them? That made no sense. He had to have them if he hoped for his share of the millions.

I sat up in bed and turned on the light. "Then it had to be Annebelle, by herself," I said aloud. She's the only one left. "But how?" For several moments, I sat motionless, staring blankly at the wall. I shook my head. No way. Annebelle couldn't be a part of it. How could she have known I was at the national park? Diane was dating WR, not Annebelle.

Besides, Annebelle had a solid alibi, the softball tournament in Jackson from the twenty-fifth through the twenty-seventh.

The old man's time of death was listed at 2:40 P.M. on

the twenty-sixth, and I had a DVD of her sitting on the bench talking with the coach, Nancy Carleton, at 1:30 P.M. Still, something was missing. I mumbled under my breath. "You got yourself a bunch of theories going nowhere, Tony."

Al Grogan is the top sleuth in my company, Blevins Security, in Austin. He mentored me, more or less, if you can classify shouting and screaming as mentoring. He was a master craftsman in the art of profanity, honing his proficiency of that questionable talent with all the dedication of a twenty-first-century Picasso or Michelangelo.

One thing Grogan always told me was that if things got too confusing, too complicated, just back out and start over.

"That's exactly what I'll do," I muttered, lying back down and turning off the light. "As soon as I catch a little sleep."

I was exhausted. Jack woke me at nine o'clock. "Hey, what the dickens happened to your pickup? The whole side's caved in."

"Go away," I mumbled, pulling the blanket over my head.

He yanked the blanket off me. "Are you going to tell me what you were up to last night? Your truck's a wreck. Are you all right?"

I rolled over and stared sleepily at him. "So? What else is new?"

Jack shook his head. "Come on down. Coffee's hot, and Alice toasted some bagels. I want to know what happened last night."

I was hungrier than I thought. While I related the events of the previous night, I ate two bagels lathered with cream cheese and washed them down with three cups of coffee.

"How does that tie together? Or does it?"

"I'm not sure, but I plan on going back over all my notes this morning. Begin at the beginning," I added, thinking of Al Grogan's declaration.

He frowned.

I explained. "The whole case is circumstantial. I need to find something to tie it together."

Jack leaned forward. "How are you going to do that?"

Gesturing to the upstairs bedroom, I replied, "I've got to go back over all my notes. I have the feeling I missed something. Cross your fingers that I can find it."

His frown deepened.

I chuckled. "I know it might sound hopeless, but believe me, I've got a pretty good idea where I'm going with it all."

"Okay. Anything I can do to help?"

"Nope. Just have Alice keep a pot of coffee perking. And," I added with a word caution, "if anyone asks, just tell them someone just sideswiped my pickup. You hear?"

"I hear."

Back in my room, I called Tom Garrett at the police station. He was in his usual truculent mood. He growled. "I was hoping you'd gone back to . . . where was it? Houston? Podunk Holler?"

I let the remark slide. "Sorry to disappoint you, but I need a favor."

"Like what?"

"I want to find out if the Tiger's Den—it's a nightclub in Shreveport—was shut down on Saturday the twenty-sixth."

His reply reeked with sarcasm. "I suppose you know that Shreveport is in Louisiana, and in case you've forgotten, this is Mississippi."

I started to tell him what he could do with that last remark, but I held my temper and innocently remarked, "You mean the Vicksburg department doesn't have a good enough relationship with a neighboring city to ask a simple question?"

One fact I had quickly learned when I first worked with the law was that cops, the long-timers, have monumental egos when it comes to their department. They can criticize it, curse it, heap abomination upon it, but they will, without hesitation, eviscerate any outsider who does the same. He remained silent a moment, then muttered an expletive. "How can I get in touch with you?"

I gave him Jack's number. "I'll be here the rest of the morning." A thought hit me. I hesitated. "And Garrett—"

"Yeah."

"One more favor. The owner of the joint is called Jumbo. I would appreciate what information you can find on him."

"You sure you don't want me to come over and tuck you in bed?"

I grinned. "I just got up. Maybe tonight. I'll call you, okay?"

He cursed again and hung up.

"Pinhead," I muttered, replacing the receiver and turning back to my desk. I spread my note cards, arranging them in chronological order beginning with the earliest date concerning the case.

The first was July 17, the date Edney called his attorney and stated he wanted to change his will. A week later, on July 24, he purportedly signed the new will. Two days later, he died in the fire. On that date, WR and Stewart claimed they were at the Tiger's Den a hundred and eighty miles away at the time of the fire, except the owner, Jumbo, stated the nightclub was closed. From July 25 through July 27, Annebelle attended a softball tournament in Jackson, some fifty miles or so east of Vicksburg. Her alibi was verified by the DVD and Nancy Carleton, the coach of the softball team, although she and the coach were not in each other's presence every hour of the day.

I continued placing cards, shifting back and forth, trying to stumble over another perspective, another angle to the case.

According to Doc Raines at the Vicksburg Auto Parts, he and JW Edney attended an antique show in Lafayette, Louisiana, two days before the fire.

Another disturbing thought hit me. Doc Raines had said Stewart ordered the naphtha a month before JW's death, yet Alice, the housekeeper, claimed Stewart and JW had reconciled only two or three weeks earlier. If her information was accurate, how could Stewart have known JW was out of cleaning fluid?

Hastily I scribbled the question on a card and placed it beside Doc Raines' card.

The card with the interview of Wilson Jenkins, the Madison Parish Ornithological Society's ex-director, I placed between the card when Edney supposedly called to inform Goggins of the new will and the card with the date he signed it.

Then I reread the cards putting Annebelle in the will and recanting the promise of the land to the Madison Parish Ornithological Society.

By now, the desktop was filled with cards.

I reread the ones concerning the autopsy. *Upon transflecting the scalp, a blunt trauma force to the left temporal area of the cranium was located.*

Thumbing through my files on the case, I retrieved the pictures of the fire. I studied the one depicting the partially consumed corpse. The body lay on its right side, the opposite side from the injury to his head.

Muttering, I went back over my theory, verbalizing just how the death occurred, hoping to discover another viewpoint that would permit more pieces of the puzzle to fall into place. "If I were at a table that suddenly ignited, I would leap backward. JW Edney did not. According to the medical examiner, he turned around, stumbled and fell to his left at the base of the table, and in the throes of suffocation, turned over to face it."

I still couldn't believe the ME's conclusion.

The only way I originally saw it, and still did, was that given the position of the body and the injury, someone struck him on the left temple, causing him to fall in the position he did.

Yet, who would Chief Hemings believe, me or the medical examiner? Who could blame him?

Suddenly I had an idea. I called Al Grogan, my ex-mentor back in Austin. I put the question to him. Without hesitation, he replied, "Don't let those southern crackers snow you, Tony. I've seen it a dozen times. If someone is unconscious and suffocating, he ain't going to turn over. He'll lay right where he fell."

My hopes soared. Right at that moment, Al could have called me every name in a sailor's book, and I would have grinned like the proverbial possum. I thanked him and hung up, tucking back that little nugget of information for the proper time to use it.

Chewing on my bottom lip, I repeated my own theory of the murder. The blow had to come from behind and from the left, which meant the killer had to be left-handed.

Annebelle? Could she be left-handed? Hastily, I slipped the DVD of the Vicksburg softball game in the player, fast forwarding to Annebelle hitting practice balls to the infielders during warmup, right-handed. I shook my head in disappointment, but I noticed something I had dismissed the first time I viewed the video. A surprising number of the players on the team were southpaws.

Then my thoughts flashed back to that day in the parlor when an enraged Stewart raised his hand to slap Annebelle. I replayed the scene in my mind. He slammed the bottle of bourbon down on the sideboard and charged Annebelle with his left arm drawn back. "I'll slap you silly," he had shouted.

Hastily, I put together the scene in the garage as it could have happened using WR. and Stewart.

WR could have distracted John Wesley Edney while Stewart approached from the rear and struck the old man in the head. That scenario fit in neatly with Doc Raine's assertion that Stewart was the one who ordered the naphtha.

Just about the time I thought the pieces might start falling together, they blew up in my face. And the piece that caused the blowup once again was named Jumbo.

I could not reconcile Jumbo trashing WR's and Stewart's alibi with his thugs showing up at the national park the previous night or whatever his dealings might be with Rebel Trucking.

Something was missing, but what?

Abruptly, the telephone rang. It was Garrett. His voice had not lost its surliness. "The Tiger's Den was wide open Saturday, and your boy, Jumbo, age fifty-one, has a rap sheet as long as your arm. Word on the street is he's related to Joe Basco, the mob boss in New Orleans. Cousin. Real name is James Franklin Harrod. He's from Jackson, Mississippi. Grew up on Oak Street, 2113."

His remark about Jumbo's home struck a familiar chord, but the significance eluded me. Joe Basco was another matter. I had been right when I guessed Jumbo was working for Basco, but why would Basco send Jumbo after me at the park? I could understand the bag of cement and the eighteen-wheelers, but the mob boss had promised to leave me alone after those two incidents. Had I gone too far? "Thanks, Garrett. I appreciate the help." I made an effort at some sort of reconciliation in case I needed more help. "I know I've been a pain, but I'd like to get together so you can see what I have."

My apology, though not abject, tempered his surliness. "Yeah. Just give me a call."

Staring at the receiver, I tried to find a path around another boulder that he had dropped in front of me. Jumbo had lied about the nightclub being closed. Why?

I noted Garrett's information on a separate card.

"Jumbo and the brothers can't be working together, but then how did he know I was at the park? And within an hour or so after I told Diane?"

I closed my eyes and groaned. "All right, Tony. It's time for a flash of inspiration."

To my surprise it came, and like most flashes of inspiration, it was so obvious, I had paid it no attention.

I practically leaped from my chair and rushed downstairs. Just as I reached the dining room, I remembered I'd left my note cards on the desk. Uttering a string of curses, I hurried back for them. After dropping them in my pocket, I paused, considering whether I should call Tom Garrett for phone records. I decided to wait. If my idea was wrong, I didn't need his mocking censure.

Chapter Twenty-seven

In the parking lot of Hair by Stewart, I rummaged through my toolbox of security gadgets and pulled out a walnut-covered box the size of a cigar box, a tap alert.

Looking up through the glass wall of his office, Stewart frowned from behind his desk when I entered his salon. He had eight chairs, and they were all in use. Half of the operators were male. I don't know much about beauty salons, but this one was bright and clean, and the air carried a pleasant fragrance. The floor was white tile and the white walls were covered with pastel flowers. Low-level chatter and giggles filled the room.

His lips curled in distaste, Stewart hurried to me, as if my coming too far into his salon would contaminate it. "What can I do for you, Mr. Boudreaux?"

I studied him a moment, his bald head, and his round face. "You're left-handed, aren't you?"

The question caught him off guard. "Huh? Yeah. Yeah, so I'm left-handed. What does that have to do with anything?"

"Just wondering." I glanced at his office. "Is there someplace we can talk privately?"

His reluctance was obvious. I prodded him. "I wouldn't be here if it wasn't important."

With a deep sigh, he nodded to his office. "In there."

He closed the door and eased into his chair. "Now, what is so important?" He glanced curiously at the box I laid on his desk.

"Two or three matters." I pulled out the note cards. "First, you told me your sister went to live with an aunt in Jackson. Right?"

"Yeah."

"You happen to remember what street she lived on?"

He frowned. "Why do you want to know that? She's dead."

Impatiently, I snapped. "Humor me, Stewart. Okay?"

He sensed the testiness in my reply. "Oak. 2222. I'll never forget that address. 2222 Oak."

"How old is your sister?"

He pondered the question a moment. "Let's see. I'm fifty-two. Annebelle must be fifty."

"How long did she live with her aunt? I mean, did she go to school in Jackson?"

"Yeah. A couple years."

What do you know, I told myself. Sherlock Boudreaux strikes again.

He frowned. "Why are you asking all this? Is she behind it all?"

I ignored his question. "Now, one more question. When I visited the Tiger's Den to attempt to verify your alibi, the owner said the nightclub was closed that night. How do you explain that?"

Stewart stared at me in wide-eyed disbelief, and his mouth dropped open. His lips opened and closed for thirty seconds before he could utter a sound. And then it was a stammering series of "Wh–wh–wh—"

"You heard me. The owner said the place was closed."

He shook his head. His jowls flopped. "Honest. We was there. That's the truth, the gospel truth. We was there from three to six."

"Why would the owner say the place was closed?"

"I don't know, but he's lying."

I didn't tell Stewart I knew Jumbo had lied. Let him stew awhile. He and his brother deserved it. To even entertain the idea of blackmailing their father with porn pictures was disgusting, but to actually take the steps to carry through with the scheme was beyond repugnant.

He leaned forward. "You believe me, don't you, Boudreaux? We sat there from three to six, drinking beer and staring at the stupid tiger with the funny legs on the wall."

"I don't know, Stewart." I rose and shook my head. "I don't know." One thing I did know now, he had been in the Tiger's Den. But whether he was there on the twenty-sixth or not was anyone's guess.

Believe it or not, my newest theory was beginning to gel. Suppressing my excitement, I nodded to his telephone. "Can I use it a moment?"

"Sure." He pushed it across the desk. I opened the box, disconnected his phone and plugged the line into the tap alert. A red light flashed. Without commenting, I disconnected the alert and plugged the line back into his phone. "Thanks," I said, rising.

He frowned. "What's that all about?"

I shook my head. "Just another little piece of the puzzle. By the way, you asked me what being left-handed had to do with anything. Remember?"

"Yeah. So?"

"It appears whoever killed your father was left-handed."

Stewart was still stammering when I left.

Served him right.

Now, all I had to do was make a short visit to WR.

Ten minutes later I parked in front of his hardware store, climbed out and tucked the tap alert under my arm.

WR was busy, so I waited at the counter. Finally, he finished with his customer and glowered at me. "You come to ask me about the Tiger's Den?"

I grinned, keeping my eye on his bottom lip. "Stewart called, huh?"

"Yeah. I don't care what anyone else says. What he said is true. We were there."

"Well, WR, maybe you were, maybe you weren't. I'm still working on the pieces."

He ran his fat hand over what few strands of hair he had remaining. "Well, when you get it all together, you'll see we're telling the truth."

To my surprise, I saw no evidence of that nervous habit of his and Jack's; running the tongue between the gums and lower lip. Could it be he was telling the truth? "That isn't why I'm here. I'd like to take a look at your telephone."

He frowned. "That's what Stewart said you did over at his place. Why?"

"Call it curiosity. You don't have to let me, but I'll just go to Chief Hemings, and he'll get a warrant."

I could see the wheels turning in his head. Should he or not? Finally, he shrugged. "Why not? I've got nothing to hide."

"Thanks. It'll only take a minute." He followed me into his office.

Opening the tap alert, I followed the same procedure I had at Hair by Stewart. Instantly, a red light flashed. Without a word, I unplugged it and closed the box.

"What's going on?" WR wore a puzzled frown.

"Nothing," I replied, reconnecting his telephone. "I just wanted to check your phone line. That's all."

"But it's got to mean something."

"It does. To me." I slid a scrap of paper across his desk and handed him a pen. "How about writing your name for me."

He shook his head. "This don't make sense."

"Trust me, WR. There's reason in my madness."

With a shrug, he scribbled his name with his right hand.

"That's all I need to know." I brushed past him for the door. "I'll be in touch."

As I climbed in my truck, I could see him still standing in the doorway to his office, scratching his head.

I was elated. I'd finally put two and two together, and for the first time since Monday night, it added up to four.

Chapter Twenty-eight

When I discovered the phone lines back at the mansion were tapped, I wasn't surprised at all.

I contacted Doc Raines for the date and time the naphtha had been ordered for JW Edney, after which I contacted Garrett for the phone records of the three siblings as well as those of the old man for July 17 through the present. Then I retired to my room to go back over my notes.

When I ran across Nancy Carleton's alibi for Annebelle, I reread her remarks, especially those referring to Annebelle's scouting the Monroe Marauders and the Beaumont Raiders.

What was so important about that game was that it took place in the same time frame as JW Edney's death. If she was scouting the game, she could not have murdered her father.

That was reason enough to drive to Jackson. I had two tasks, first to visit the school that Annebelle attended her two years in Jackson, and second to pick up another DVD, this one of the Beaumont Raiders and the Monroe Marauders. If she scouted the game, perhaps she would be in the video. And if she was, my theory was shot.

Annebelle had attended two schools in Jackson, the last year of junior high and the first of high school. In the 1965

Jackson Bulldog Annual, I thumbed through the freshman pictures until I found Annebelle's picture, and two pages farther, the one for which I had hoped, James Franklin Harrod, better known as Jumbo.

So far, so good.

Then I visited Coach Barnes to purchase a DVD of the Marauders and Raiders. He recognized me. "I was wondering how to get in touch with you."

I frowned. "Me? Why?"

"You bought a DVD the other day." I nodded, and he continued. "I learned later that batch had some editing problems. I forgot which one you bought. If it's one of the bad ones, I'll give you a corrected DVD."

I started to dismiss his offer, but then figured I might as well take it. "Thanks," I told him, and minutes later I was on the road back to Vicksburg with the corrected DVD plus a DVD of the Marauders and Raiders.

I read somewhere that to make a fortune, you must have some assistance from Fate. I could paraphrase the axiom and say to make a solid case, you can always use some assistance from Fate.

And that afternoon, Fate smiled on me, twice; once when I was given a corrected DVD, and second when a Mississippi State Patrol pulled me over and issued me a warning for driving too fast. Grateful for the warning, I effusively thanked him.

"We've cracked down the last few weeks," he replied. "We want you to get home alive."

The last twenty miles, I drove under the seventy-mile speed limit.

By one o'clock, I was back in Vicksburg. To my surprise, the phone records I had requested were on the coffee table in the parlor. Maybe Garrett wasn't the jerk I thought he was.

I had previously believed that if one of the three siblings was the killer, and if the act was carried out by a left-handed individual, then the killer had to be Stewart. Yet, thanks to the contradiction between Jumbo not supporting their alibi and his thugs attacking me at the military park, there was no way I could put together an unbroken chain of evidence linking Stewart and WR to their father's death despite the preponderance of evidence pointing to him and his brother.

If the killer wasn't Stewart or WR, it had to be Annebelle, but she was not a southpaw. I had seen the DVD with her hitting practice balls to the players, right-handed.

Or maybe she was ambidextrous. Maybe WR was.

I shook my head in frustration and inserted the Monroe and Beaumont fast-pitch softball game in the DVD, hoping that Annebelle Edney would be nowhere in sight. That could mean she slipped away at 1:30, raced home, killed the old man, then returned in time for the 5:30 game.

What I saw dashed cold water on my little theory. In the first inning as the lead-off hitter came to the plate, the camera panned the spectators, and there was Annebelle as big as life. I replayed the scene several times just to be sure.

Fast forwarding through the remainder of the game, I paused each time the spectators were panned. I failed to see Annebelle again, but I had to reluctantly concede that the camera had panned different segments of the spectators. The game ended with the Marauders winners, six to four. In the last pan at the end of the game, I spotted her once again.

I replayed the video.

The bleachers on which the spectators sat were aluminum, permitting a view of the parking lot behind. At the beginning of the last inning, a blue pickup drove behind the bleachers. I replayed the clip several times. I couldn't tell the make, but I remembered the blue Ford F150 pickup parked in front of the old man's house when Jack and I drove in on Monday.

I wondered if the pickup on the tape could be Annebelle's. Sure, she was sitting in the stands at the end of the game, but still, I hadn't seen her from about 1:40 until after 5. Maybe my theory wasn't so far off base after all.

The time of JW Edney's death was 2:40. I did some fast calculating. There was still time. She could have left Jackson at 1:40, committed the murder at 2:40, and got back to Jackson by 5. I just needed proof she wasn't at the game the entire time.

And she could have been the one to order the naphtha, not Stewart. Their voices were similar.

A wild idea hit me. It was a long shot, but sometimes long shots pay off. I called Tom Garrett.

His temperament had mellowed somewhat, having all the vitriol of a rattlesnake. "Yeah?"

"Garrett, it's me, Boudreaux. Do you have any connections with the state highway patrol?"

"What's on your mind now?"

I held my tongue. "Just tell me."

"Some. Why?"

"Check for a ticket issued to Annebelle Edney on the twenty-sixth between the times of one-thirty P.M. and five-thirty."

He muttered a curse. "Look, I'm getting tired of this nonsense, Boudreaux. You're just wasting everybody's time. Why don't you do like the rest of us and accept the medical examiner's findings, that JW Edney died by a fire he caused?"

Suppressing the peals of anger ringing in my ears, I held my temper. Obviously, Garrett had paid no attention to the death, nor, I reminded myself, should he. The ME declared it accidental. "Listen carefully, Detective. The body lay on its right side at the base of the table. Now, if the fracture to the skull was caused by the fall, the injury would be on the right side. Correct?"

He snorted. "Yeah."

"Edney's skull was fractured on the left, indicating that a left-handed person stood behind him and struck him on the left temple. A blow on the left temple would have knocked the old man to the floor, on his right side. You agree?"

Garrett did not speak for several seconds.

"Garrett? You still there?"

He snarled. "Yeah. Yeah, I'm here. Go on. So what did the medical examiner say? You did ask him about that, didn't you?"

"He surmised that when the sparks exploded, JW Edney spun from the table, stumbled and fell to his left, and then while he was unconscious and suffocating, he rolled over to face the table. But," I added, trying to sound much more authoritative than I felt, "anyone with experience in smoke inhalation deaths will tell you that it is impossible for an unconscious person who is asphyxiating to roll over." I paused. "That's why I say this was murder and not an accident."

Garrett remained silent for several seconds, but I could hear the seasoned lawman's brain working. I hoped he was seasoned enough to not let personalities influence him. Finally, he said, "All right. Tell me again what you need."

I repeated my request.

"You're playing a long shot here, Boudreaux. Besides, a search like that could take days."

"If they inputted it in the database, it won't."

He hesitated, then, "All right. Anything to get you back to Podunk Holler."

Before he hung up, I said, "Hey, thanks for the phone records. We couldn't have done it any faster back in Podunk Holler."

Garrett was still cursing when I hung up.

Chapter Twenty-nine

After hanging up, I inserted the corrected DVD in the player. I kept my fingers crossed. And there she was, Annebelle Edney, right in front of my eyes, hitting balls to the team, and, to my stunned surprise, left-handed.

Excited, I hit the pause button and fumbled with the phone, placing a call to Matt Barnes in Jackson. When he answered, I blurted out, "You gave me a corrected copy of the Vicksburg game. What was wrong with the initial editing?"

"I thought I told you."

"No, no. What was it? You didn't tell me." My words tumbled over one another.

"No big deal. We accidentally reversed the images."

For a moment, I was speechless. I had not even thought of such a possibility. Then I remembered the number of southpaws on the team in the first DVD. That should have told me something, but the idea never occurred to me. "You mean, you reversed the images?" I knew I sounded like a dummy, but I was too stunned to ask an intelligent question. I repeated myself. "You reversed the images?"

He laughed. "Yeah. Reversed. You know, flip-flopped, backwards. They're straight on the new one though."

*   *   *

I clung to my newest theory, hoping to prove it when I talked to Annebelle. To do that, I had to be sure I asked the right questions.

Spreading the telephone records and note cards on the desk, I jotted several questions beginning with the signing of the will on July 24. I hesitated. For some reason, the date leaped out at me. I studied the card, then those on either side, one of which indicated that on July 17 JW Edney purportedly called his attorney to instruct a new will; the other had the assertion from Doc Raines down at Vicksburg Auto Parts that two days before JW's death, they had attended an antique car show in Lafayette, Louisiana.

Then, like a sixteen-pound sledgehammer, it hit me between the eyes. The nagging thought that had kept worrying at me all week, telling me I had missed something. There it was, plain as the proverbial nose on my face.

I muttered a soft curse. "The missing piece." How could I have been so thick-witted. "Why didn't I see that?" I muttered. The day he attended a car show with Doc Raines two hundred and fifteen miles to the south in Lafayette is the day he was purportedly signing the new will in lawyer Goggins' office!

I opened my copy of the new will and checked the date. Sure enough, July 24. My fingers fumbled from the excitement coursing through my veins as I picked up the card dated the twenty-fourth and reread it. According to Annebelle on Monday evening after the heirs met with Goggins, she told WR that her father had called her on the twenty-fourth just after lunch to tell he signed the new will. Impossible!

"Slow down, Tony," I muttered. "Think. Surely, Annebelle and Goggins aren't so stupid as to claim her father signed the new will on a day he was out of town. What if they hadn't known he was out of town?"

Hastily, I called Doc Raines at the Vicksburg Auto Parts. "Are you certain that you and JW were in Lafayette on the twenty-fourth and fifth?"

"Absolutely," he replied. "I was just going by myself, but at the last moment, I called JW. He'd planned to stay home and work on his cars, but he just said, 'What the heck,' and came along."

"Spur of the moment, huh?"

Doc laughed. "Yep. Didn't tell anyone. In fact, on the drive down, he mentioned that he needed to call his house-keeper when we reached Lafayette so she wouldn't worry."

I grinned with satisfaction, thanked him, and hung up. On impulse, I headed for the kitchen where I found Alice.

"Yes, sir. Can I get something for you?"

"One question, Alice. Last Friday, the twenty-fourth. Did Mr. Edney happen to get a phone call from his daughter?"

She frowned, then nodded. "Annebelle. Yes, sir. I told her he was out, but likely he would soon be back. A few hours later, just before I left for the day, he called telling me he was in Lafayette. I tried to call Miss Annebelle back, but there was no answer." She hesitated. "Is everything all right?"

"Is everything all right?" I laughed and picked her up and swung her around. "Everything is perfect, Alice, just perfect."

Back in my bedroom, I stared at the cards on my desk. Now all I had to do was confirm the evidence, and I had my killer.

At that moment, the phone rang. It was Garrett. "You got lucky, Boudreaux," he said, the hostile edge gone from his voice. "A warning ticket was given to Annebelle Edney at four-fifty P.M. between mile markers thirty-four and thirty-five on I-20 on July 26."

I shouted into the receiver. "Fantastic!"

"Hey! What the—"

I hastily apologized. "Sorry, Garrett. I didn't mean to yell in your ear. That little tidbit just about nails the lid on her."

He hesitated. "What are you talking about?"

"Annebelle Edney."

"She killed her old man? I don't believe it."

Quickly, I detailed what I had discovered.

Garrett wasn't impressed. "A good lawyer could tear it to pieces."

"Maybe. But, what if I can get either Goggins or Annebelle to admit it?"

"You'll never get a lawyer to admit it, and she would just turn around later and deny saying it."

"Not if you were there."

For a moment, a pregnant silence greeted my ears. "What do you have in mind?"

"What if I met Annebelle someplace where you could hear her admission?"

"Like where?"

I pondered the question a moment. Then, I thought of the perfect spot. "Out at the military park. There's a site with a cave. Thayer's Approach. Site number six, I think. You could get there ahead of time. From what I read, the cave's at the bottom of the stairs. You hide inside. I'll meet her just in front of the cave."

"How are you going to get her out there?"

"I've been thinking about that. She might need a little nudge. I think I can give it to her."

He hesitated. Finally, "Sounds just dumb enough to work. If that'll help get you back to Podunk Holler, I'll jump right in. What time?"

"I'll let you know. I'll contact her. Try to set it up for around four."

Hastily slipping the cards into my shirt pocket, I hurried downstairs, anxious to pay William Goggins a visit.

Goggins greeted me as he would any prospective client, solicitous of my well-being, considerate of my intentions, and concerned about my progress. He studied me intently. "I heard through the grapevine about the accident in your pick-up. I hope you weren't injured." The worried look in his eyes did not reflect his concerned words.

I relaxed. Jack had stayed with our cover story. "News travels fast around here."

His expression remained unchanged as he chuckled and gestured to the red leather chair. "You know how small towns are. Nothing exciting ever happens. WR told me about the damage to your pickup. If I'm not mistaken, he learned of it from Jack. Please. Have a seat. Tell me, how is the investigation going? Well, I hope."

I nodded. "As well as can be expected."

"So, what do you need from me?"

Behind his smooth façade, I sensed a tense wariness, like an animal bunched and waiting to leap. "Not much," I replied casually. "Just want to verify the date on the new will. I had made a note of it, but—" I shrugged. "You know how it goes. I misplaced it."

The wariness faded. "No problem," he replied with a voice as smooth as honey. He picked up his phone and requested his secretary to bring him the Edney file.

She remained standing by his desk as he flipped the portfolio open and retrieved the will. "Here, Mr. Boudreaux," he said, opening the document and handing it to me. "See for yourself. At the bottom. By his signature."

"I see. July 24. One-forty-three P.M. That's odd." I looked up at him. "Are you sure that was the correct date?"

He bristled. "Certainly. For the sake of our clients and their welfare, we cannot afford mistakes."

I apologized profusely. "I didn't mean to offend you, Mr. Goggins. I probably misunderstood another witness who claimed JW was out of town on that day. I'll doublecheck my information."

He stiffened, then relaxed. Clearing his throat, he replied, "Who might that be, Mr. Boudreaux?"

"I'd rather not say. If it was just a mistake, I wouldn't want to embarrass the individual. You understand."

He nodded. "Of course. I'll check our records also. Mistakes can happen. My secretary might have entered the wrong date."

She shot him a brief, but withering look.

He continued. "I can check our appointment books if you wish." He dragged the tip of his tongue over his lips.

I handed him the will. "No. I'm sure the other witness was mistaken." I nodded to the Edney file. "Do you mind if I take a look at his file?"

His fingers tightened about the file. "May I ask why?"

With a disarming smile, I replied, "Certainly. I'm looking for something, but I don't know what. I don't know if I would recognize it even if I saw it."

He glanced uncomfortably at his secretary, then offered me the file. "By all means."

I turned to the beginning of the file. Within seconds, I found that for which I had hoped, several follow-up letters for various purchases over the last four decades, but not one for the new will. That was all I needed to confirm that Goggins was part of the scheme.

Closing the file, I slid it across his desk. "Thanks." I rose and offered my hand. "I do appreciate your time."

A frown wrinkled his forehead. "Did you find what you were looking for?"

"Nope. Thanks again."

His secretary opened the office door for me. I glanced back as she closed it, just in time to see lawyer William Goggins punching in a number on the phone. I crossed my fingers, hoping he was calling the killer. If he was, then the first step in my plan had been successful.

Next stop, Annebelle Edney.

Chapter Thirty

My telephone call did not surprise Annebelle, nor did I expect it would.

I came right to the point. "We need to talk. As soon as possible this afternoon."

With an indifferent tone, she said, "I have a route to complete."

"It would be in your interest to make the time, Annebelle. If I turn what I've found over to Chief Hemings, the only route you'll be running is around a dirty six-by-nine cell at Parchmann Prison for Women before you ride the needle."

She said nothing for several moments. I held my breath. She had to know of my visit to Goggins, and he had to have told her about my questioning the date on the will. Finally, she said, "When?"

"Four o'clock. At the military park. Thayer's Approach. I'll be at the bottom of the stairs."

"Why out there?"

"No one around to hear us."

Several more seconds of silence elapsed. Finally, "All right. Four o'clock."

I looked at my watch. It was two. I called Garrett. "Be there early. I'll wait at the gate for her, then we'll come down together."

Garrett growled. "I hope you know what you're doing. This better not be a waste of my time."

"Just be there."

Annebelle was on time. I climbed out of my pickup in the parking area at site six, Thayer's Approach. She parked her Riverside Bread truck next to the curb across the paved road.

Thayer's Approach is a deep ravine fifty yards wide and almost four hundred in length with a shallow gully at the bottom cut by runoff rain, narrow enough one can step over it. The west side of the ravine was a two-hundred-yard open stretch sloping upward at a forty-five-degree angle to the rim of a redoubt once manned by Confederate troops. During the battle, General Thayer's Union boys made a bloody, but unsuccessful attempt to scale the slope under the withering gunfire from the Twenty-sixth Louisiana Redoubt.

A flight of concrete stairs led to the bottom of the ravine. To the side of the stairs was a concrete cave with an arched entrance, constructed by Thayer's forces as protection against the weapons of the Confederates on the slope towering over them.

When Annebelle climbed from her truck, I started down the stairs, casting a hasty glance in the direction of the cave. I grinned to myself when I spotted movement back in the shadows. Garrett was waiting.

At the base of the stairs, I looked around, and my heart started hammering in my chest like the proverbial jackhammer. Annebelle was halfway down the stairs, and behind her came all six-foot-four and three hundred pounds of Jumbo.

Instinctively, I took a few steps backward.

She stopped a few feet in front of me. She was a couple inches shorter than I, but probably had me by ten or twenty pounds. She jammed her fists in her hips and stared at me narrowly. "Well, what's so important?"

I hadn't planned on her bringing Jumbo along. At that moment, I wished I had never met Jack Edney, but now it was too late. I glanced at Jumbo. "How much does he know?"

"Everything."

Taking a deep breath and slowly releasing it, I said, "You know why I came to Vicksburg. Well, I found what I was looking for. Good news for me, bad for you."

"Oh?" She arched an eyebrow.

I had no hard proof, but I was convinced that Annebelle was the only one who could have put a tap on her brothers' lines. I tried a bluff, hoping she'd fall for it. "I wasn't sure about you until I discovered you had put a phone tap on your brothers' phones. Once I learned that, everything fell into place. That, and now seeing Jumbo answers several questions that had puzzled me. Joe Basco ordered Jumbo to send the cement man and the eighteen-wheelers after me, and you had Jumbo send the bombers and those two thugs out at the park after me. Probably even the Cadillac and the shooter."

She laughed, a drawn-out sneer. "So?"

I grinned to myself. She had fallen for my bluff. Her calm acceptance of the accusation told me exactly what I wanted to know, that she had planted the bugs and was behind the last few attempts on my life. "So, Jumbo there was the go-between for the land deal with you and Basco as well as doing your dirty work."

"Prove it."

"Don't think I can't. I've come up with more than enough to put you in Parchmann, but when I considered all the ins and outs of turning the evidence over to the police, I began to wonder whether you might be smart enough to take on a partner—a silent partner, of course. Once WR and Stewart end up riding the needle, you'll have all the money you can spend. And I'm not greedy."

She said nothing. She continued eyeing me with no trace of emotion. "Why should I?"

I glanced over her shoulder at Jumbo. "I can think of two good reasons. Life in prison is one. A needle up your arm is another."

She sneered. "You really think I killed John, don't you?"

"I know you did. Your first mistake was that day in the

parlor when you told Stewart 'at least, I have an alibi.' I couldn't help wondering later just how you knew their alibis wouldn't hold up unless you had set it up yourself. You hired someone to play the lawyer with the porn. And Jumbo there helped you by claiming the Tiger's Den was closed on the twenty-sixth, which destroyed your brothers' alibis."

"You can't prove a thing."

"No? I can prove you and Jumbo have a history back to high school. I can prove there was no new will, the one you claimed you learned of when your father called on the twenty-fourth and said he was going to his attorney's to sign the new will."

"He did call."

"He couldn't. He was in Lafayette, Louisiana."

Her eyes narrowed. "Don't make me laugh. When I talked to him the day before he told me he was going to work on his cars before he went to Goggins' office."

"No. You made all that up. He didn't call you. His phone records don't show any call to your number on the twenty-third, but they do show one from you to him."

She glanced around nervously. "It's your word against mine. You can't prove I said he called me."

Clucking my tongue, I replied, "Wrong again, Annebelle. WR and Jack were there. That's the night WR asked you how you knew you had been put back in the will. Remember? They heard you say JW called you."

She glared at me, hate boiling in her eyes. "So I got my words mixed up. Sue me!"

I continued. "JW couldn't have signed that will because he was in Lafayette with Doc Raines the day you and your friend Goggins claimed the new will was signed."

She nibbled at her bottom lip. "They're mistaken."

I kept glancing at Jumbo, expecting him to erupt at any second. I continued. "That isn't all. You're the one who ordered the naphtha for your father, not Stewart."

"You don't know what you're talking about."

Shaking my head, I couldn't suppress an amused grin. "You can deny it all you want, but I have the phone records showing you called the Vicksburg Auto Parts at the very moment the order was placed. Your voice is similar to Stewart's. Doc Raines thought it was Stewart who called."

"It was Stewart."

"No. Neither his home phone nor salon phone called the parts house. Besides, he had no way of knowing JW needed cleaning fluid. The two hadn't spoken in months." I paused, then added, "What do you think Goggins is going to do when the Mississippi Board of Attorneys starts action to strip him of his license? I'll tell you what. He'll sing like one of those Kentucky Warblers your father wanted to save."

Annebelle licked her lips, but kept her cold eyes fixed on mine. "I couldn't have killed John. I was in Jackson, at the softball tournament. Nancy Carleton will swear to it," she said smugly. "I might have called about the naphtha, but I was fifty miles away when John died."

"I know you were in Jackson, but Nancy Carleton can't swear she was with you from one-thirty to five-fifteen or so on Saturday the twenty-sixth."

"I was scouting a ball game—the Monroe Marauders and the Beaumont Raiders."

I arched an eyebrow. Her face grew red. "Who won?"

She hesitated. "The Marauders."

"What was the score?"

"I don't remember," she said, shaking her head.

"Come on, Annebelle. It was only last Saturday."

For several seconds she concentrated. "Oh, yeah. Now I remember. Six, four, Marauders."

I clucked my tongue. "If I were still a school teacher, I'd have to give you an A on that answer. You were there at the beginning and end. You're in the video."

A smug grin played over her face. "I told you."

Then I hit her between the eyes with the one piece of evidence that tied the case up. "Yes, but what you didn't tell me was that at four-fifty that day, you were parked between mile markers thirty-four and thirty-five on I-twenty getting a warning ticket from the Mississippi Highway Patrol. You just had enough time to get back before the five-thirty game."

She glanced at Jumbo, who was staring at me with the cold black eyes of a shark. From the blank expression in his eyes, I couldn't tell if any of this was registering with him or not.

I just hoped Garrett was getting an earful. "Jumbo there is Joe Basco's cousin. Like I said, you and Jumbo go back to middle school and high school in Jackson. It was through Jumbo you were going to arrange to sell the thousand acres to Basco and help you discredit your brothers' alibis."

She remained silent, her eyes seething with hate, her face flushed. She appeared ready to explode.

I pushed her further. "You made a poor choice with your lawyer. Your father had a habit of following up any major decision with a letter confirming the decision. There are dozens of such letters in his file at the attorney's, but there's not one letter confirming the last will. And if JW Edney actually requested a new will, a letter would be in the file."

"Goggins probably misplaced it."

I grinned. "Nice try, but the fact of the matter is, he had no idea about the letters. Still doesn't, nor do you." Keeping one eye on Jumbo, I continued. "But, you know what really made me realize you were the one?"

She sneered. "Keep guessing."

"Batting practice in Jackson. I had eliminated you as a suspect because the killer had to be left-handed. On the first DVD, you were batting right-handed. Then I saw the corrected version of the DVD." Her face tightened, her eyes narrowed. She knew exactly what I was going to say. "I saw you hitting practice balls to the players, but this time, it was left-handed. That was the only way your father could have received the injury to his head. I don't exactly know what took place in the garage that day, but I'm guessing you found your father working on one of his cars and maybe you told him you'd come to straighten out the problems between you two or something like that. Whatever the reason, you were standing behind him when you struck him. Then you set the fire and raced back to Jackson. Unfortunately for you, the highway patrol stopped you."

Suddenly, she jumped back and pulled a silver-plated revolver from inside her shirt. "Get back!"

Jumbo stepped aside, looking at her, waiting for her instructions. Glaring at me, she ignored him. In a strident voice, she said, "You're crazy if you think I'll share anything with you. I've been through too much to get my hands on what I rightfully deserve. With all I had to put up with from that man, I deserve more, but I'll settle for my share." She took a step backward. Her tone grew muted, almost gentle. "I won't, I can't let you stop that." She paused and continued. "Jumbo here has been a big help. I couldn't have done it without him. Still, a person doesn't need any excess baggage." She gave him a broad smile.

The dumb lug grinned at her like a little puppy for a moment, then a puzzled frown wrinkled his forehead.

The next few seconds seemed like hours.

Without warning, she spun and fired three slugs into Jumbo's heart. His eyes popped open in stunned surprise. He grabbed at his chest with his two plate-sized hands and opened his mouth, but no words rolled over his trembling lips.

As soon as she began firing, I turned and leaped down the ravine into the shallow gully. From somewhere, I heard Garrett shout, "Throw down the gun, or I'll shoot!"

Gunfire filled the air. I tried to force myself deeper into the gully. In less than five seconds, the gunfire ceased. I looked up to see Garrett staggering from the cave, and Annebelle disappearing over the top of the stairs.

Jumbo lay on the ground, dead.

Chapter Thirty-one

Annebelle escaped.

Garrett had taken a slug in his right shoulder and one in his left foot. He was doing well when I left him at the hospital. I think the tonic that really pumped him up was the realization I was finally leaving Vicksburg.

Next morning at the police station, I spent a few hours going over all the evidence I had collected with another detective. "Tell Garrett I'll come visit him." I grinned. "That'll make his day."

"I'll do that. By the way, he wanted to know what gave you the idea of Annebelle Edney getting a warning ticket?"

With a grin, I explained. "I got one. I figured she had to drive over the speed limit to make sure she was back in time for the last game. Luckily, I guessed right."

On the way back to Jack's, I finally came to the only logical explanation of why Annebelle had tried to place the blame on her brothers. I didn't want to believe anyone could be so cold and unfeeling, but for the life of me, I could come up with no other justification. Stewart was gay; WR divorced. If by some chance, they received the death penalty for the death of their father, as their sister she would inherit half of their shares of the estate with the remainder going to Jack.

I shivered at her plans. Annebelle plotted not only the death of her father, but ultimately those of WR and Stewart, both of whom had coldly planned to blackmail their own father with pornography.

What a merciless, calloused family. Poor Jack.

Back at the Edney mansion, my eyes widened in surprise when I spotted a brand new white 2004 Silverado pickup parked in front of the house, complete with toolbox in the back.

Inside, the three brothers were in a subdued mood, sobered by the realization that their sister had murdered their father.

"No sign of her?" Stewart asked.

"Bulletins are out around the country. Sooner or later, the law will find her, if Joe Basco doesn't find her first. If you hear from her, don't get involved. The law will nail your skin to the wall, and Basco will throw you to the 'gators."

Jack frowned. "Basco?"

"Mob boss in New Orleans. Jumbo's cousin."

Stewart whistled. "I've heard about him. Nothing good."

WR sipped his bourbon. "How did you figure all this out, Boudreaux?"

I wasn't anxious to go into detail, so I brushed it off. "Luck for the most part. Of course, I know you're disappointed because the land south of town goes to the Madison Parish birdwatchers."

Stewart grimaced. "Well, I won't lie and say I'm not disappointed, but John left us enough. I'm satisfied."

"Yeah." WR nodded "I was worried though, especially when you told us the Tiger's Den was closed that Saturday."

With a crooked grin, I winked at Jack. "Annebelle had it stacked against you boys. She knew exactly what she was doing. To stay on top of what you two were planning, she put a tap on your phones."

WR gaped. "You mean—"

"Yeah. She recorded every call you received." I paused, then with a crooked grin said, "Every call Diane made to you, WR, your sister intercepted. That's how she knew what was going on. Then she called Jumbo."

WR looked at me a moment, then his cheeks flushed, and he dropped his gaze to the floor.

"But like I said, Annebelle put together a clever plan. Through Jumbo, she had arranged to sell the land to Joe Basco. Jumbo was Basco's cousin."

Jack shook his head. "I still can't imagine our sister doing that. Why would she try to put the blame on WR and Stewart?"

WR leaned forward. "Yeah. Why did she do that, Boudreaux?"

I knew the answer, but I kept it to myself. What good would it do for them to realize the depth of their sister's hatred? I shrugged. "Who knows why people do a lot of things?"

WR arched an eyebrow. "What about Basco? I don't suppose he's too happy about not getting the land."

Raising an eyebrow, Stewart said, "He's probably going to be a lot unhappier when he hears about his cousin, Jumbo, getting killed."

We all grew silent, knowing that when Joe Basco was unhappy, he would take care of whomever or whatever caused the unhappiness. Mentally I ticked off the number of attempts on my life in the last few days. Seven or eight of them. If I'd been a cat, now was the time to start worrying.

The fact that Joe Basco was probably unhappy and that I wasn't a cat was reason enough for me to load up my new truck and get out of Vicksburg.

At that moment, the phone rang. Stewart answered it, glanced at me and nodded. "Yeah. He's right here." He held the receiver out to me.

I grimaced as I listened to the chilling news. "I understand. And thanks, Chief. I do appreciate all your help." Slowly, I replaced the receiver.

Jack spoke up. "What did the cops say?"

Clearing my throat, I replied, "They want you boys down at the morgue."

WR stepped forward. Brows knit, his voice trembling, he whispered, "Annebelle?"

All I could do was nod. I didn't have the heart to tell them that Annebelle Edney had been found on a narrow dirt road south of Vicksburg; hands tied behind her back, her feet tied, she had been shot in the back of the head. Executioners, unknown.

Truth is, I was struck by the irony that Fate always seems to deal out in its poker games. Annebelle Edney planned to eliminate her brothers for their share of the estate. With her death, they inherited her share.

Makes you wonder.

Later, Jack looked on as I tossed my sports bag in the rear of the pickup. Hooked to the rear of the pickup was a rented lowboy trailer with a 1925 Model T Runabout tied down. I glanced around at him. "So you're going back to Austin?" I looked up at the old mansion. "You sure?"

"Yeah." He whistled softly, glancing back at the two-story house. "This isn't home anymore. Oh, I'll come back for visits, but this isn't home anymore."

"What about the house?"

He shrugged. "Alice can live in it. We decided she deserves more than John left her. It's hers as long as she wants to stay here. We're each giving her a hundred thousand. And an extra hundred thousand from Annebelle's share."

I looked around at the crunch of gravel and saw the black Cadillac pulling in the drive. The big car stopped in front of us. I froze, my heart lodged in my throat. The window hissed down.

Sal Tonanno peered up at me, his thin lips twisted in a sneer. I waited for the muzzle of the hit piece to poke out. "Joe wanted that land."

I gulped and nodded.

"But, he says he's satisfied that Jumbo got his payback."

It took me a few moments to absorb the meaning of his words. I'd figured Basco was behind Annebelle's execution. Now I knew for certain. Nodding slowly, I said, "I had nothing against Mr. Basco."

Tonanno grinned, but it was cold and chilling. "He knows." The window hissed up.

As they drove away, I turned to Jack. "Well, if you're going, hop in. Let's hit the road. We've got a long ways to go."

He started back to the house. "Let me grab my bags and tell WR and Stewart good-bye." He paused and frowned at me. "You want to tell them anything?"

I shook my head slowly. "No offense, Jack, but if I ever see them or this town again, it'll be too soon."

Driving south on Washington Street to I-20, we passed Casper's Steak and Shrimp House. I thought of Diane who, in keeping WR informed of my plans, had unknowingly been responsible for several of the attempts on my life. Taking a deep breath, I sighed. Like WR and Stewart, if I ever saw her again, it would be too soon.

Jack drove me crazy all the way home. When he wasn't asking question after question about the investigation, he was jabbing that arm scratcher in and out of his cast with all the vigor a wildcatter explores for oil. For the most part, I ignored him. I was too busy figuring out just how much groveling I would have to do to get Janice to forgive me.